"Wild women don't get no blues."

IDA COX, *Raisin' Cain Review*

"It was a high counsel that I once heard given to a young person, 'Always do what you are afraid to do.'"

RALPH WALDO EMERSON

"Friends describe me as someone who likes to dance along the edge of the roof. I try to encourage young women to be willing to take risks. . . ."

WILMA MANKILLER, *Mankiller*

Dancing on the Edge
of the Roof

Dancing on the Edge of the Roof

Sheila Williams

One World
Ballantine Books • New York

A One World Book
Published by The Ballantine Publishing Group

www.ballantinebooks.com/one/

Library of Congress Cataloging-in-Publication Data is available
from the publisher upon request.

ISBN 0-345-45930-X

Cover design by Dreu Pennington-McNeil
Cover illustration by Christopher B. Clarke

Text design by Debbie Glasserman

Manufactured in the United States of America

First Edition: November 2002

1 3 5 7 9 10 8 6 4 2

This book is dedicated to the memory of Patricia Singleton Sabia, whose spirit always danced.

Acknowledgments

I have been told that patience is a virtue, but I never believed it until I met two phenomenal ladies who have patience in abundance and were gracious enough to share it with me. Many, many thanks to my agent, Alison Picard, for her support, faith, and encouragement. She believed even when I didn't. Grateful thanks are also extended to my editor, Shauna Summers, for her enthusiasm, support, and guidance—thank you.

I started writing because I couldn't think of anything better to do with a pencil and paper and because I loved to listen to and tell stories. Fortunately for me, I had family and friends patient enough to bear with me over these many, many years! Thanks to all of you! I am indebted to my mother, Myrtle, my "favorite" sister, Claire, my friends, and especially to my children, Bethany and Kevin, who kept asking me, "Mom, is that book finished yet?"

And, finally, thanks to Bruce, who is always there.

Dancing on the Edge
of the Roof

My life has been one long, muddy road after another. Potholes and puddles, a little sunshine here and there, mostly rain, though. Never anything remarkable. Nothing to write home about. But I want to change all that. I want to start over: change myself *and* my life. Now I don't want disasters and plagues. And I know the gods won't let me have a smooth road with sunshine every day either. I want to be fair about this.

But once, just once, I'd like some drama in my life, an adventure, with a dash of romance thrown in. I want a life worth writing about. I want to dance on the edge of the roof. Only up there can you hear the thunder and see the rainbows.

Juanita Louis

Chapter One

When I was forty-two years old, I decided to run away from home. Just pack up and go.

Wouldn't take dishes or nothin', no "household goods," stuff like that. Just my own stuff. What I could get into two suitcases.

Wasn't runnin' away exactly, just movin' on. I wanted to see things I'd never seen before, go places different from here.

I had been here too long.

Wasn't nothin' happenin' here. Not a damn thing.

Sometimes, you hear people say they want to find themselves. Well, I didn't need to do that. I knew where I was. That was the problem.

When I was a kid, I watched the Popeye cartoons on Saturday mornin' before my momma waked up. Swee' Pea, the baby, he was my favorite. He would feel like he wasn't bein' treated right, so he would tie up all his things in a bandanna (like the ones my son Rashawn wears on his head now) and put it on a pole and crawl away, him in his pjs. And he'd see monsters and China and the ocean— the exciting things he'd never seen before.

It was like a big adventure.

That's what I wanted. A big adventure, all my own.

Now, you know there was a lot workin' against me. I'm not what you call educated or nothin' like that. I ain't never been nowhere, don't have much of a life as it is. Got a COTA bus life—I go where the bus go: to work, to the carry-out, then home.

And I'm not the kinda woman that you would think could have adventures. I'm not brave or smart. Not pretty or important. I ain't nobody you ever heard of. Ha! I'll *never* be anybody you heard of!

And to most folks, I ain't much. But that's OK. I was smart enough to know that I couldn't stay here. Couldn't keep living the same old piece of life, doing the same old thing. Somebody said "life is not a dress rehearsal." I know what that means.

You don't get a second chance.

I think it's time to leave. Juanita's great adventure.

Even if I don't get very far, it will still be farther than *I've* been.

If Swee' Pea can have an adventure, then so can I.

Now, I didn't come to this way of thinking overnight. It took a long time.

"Momma?"

Bertie's voice took me out of my daydream.

"Momma!"

"Momma in there?" I heard my daughter yell back to her brother.

"Bertie, she *in* there," Rashawn yelled back. "She just

writin' in that notebook again, that's all. You know how
she gets."

"Momma, you in there, or what?"

Bertie's pounding was starting to get on my nerves.

"Whatchu want, Bertie? And quit banging on my door!
You gonna tear it down?"

"Sorry, Momma," Bertie said. But she didn't sound like
she was sorry. "Momma, can you keep Teishia for me? Me
and Cheryl goin' to the Do Drop."

"Then you and Cheryl needs to take Teishia with you,"
I said. "I want some peace and quiet tonight."

"Aw, Momma! I ain't been out in two days!" she whined.
I hate it when Bertie whines.

"I won't be gone long, I promise," she lied. "Besides,
Teishia'll be good. She go right to sleep."

I sighed. That was the right word. Sigh . . . I closed my
notebook and went to put it away.

"Bertie, the last time you said that, that baby kept me
up till two. And you and Cheryl didn't come home till
mornin'." I opened the bedroom door. My daughter was
standing there, dressed and ready to go. Teishia was sitting in the middle of the floor, playing with a Bic lighter. I
ran over to her and snatched it away.

"Bertie, you a fool or what? You got t' watch that child
every minute! She mighta set herself—and us—on fire! And
put these up!" I clicked the lighter. The flame jumped up
an inch.

Bertie rolled her eyes like she thought *I* was stupid.

"Girl, you roll those eyes like that again, you be pickin'
them up off the floor!"

"Momma, she *only* a baby. She can't work it."

"And *you* a fool." I stashed the lighter in my robe pocket.

"You gonna keep her or not?" Bertie's hand was on her hip, and she was getting a definite attitude. I woulda got one with her but I had just come off a ten-hour shift at the hospital. I was tired. All I wanted was for this baby to go to sleep so I could relax. I could always jump an attitude with Bertie some other time.

"She better go to sleep," I told Bertie. Teishia stuck one fat finger in her mouth.

Bertie lit out that door so fast, it made your head spin.

She left an empty Doritos bag, four Coke cans, and a full ashtray behind her. Not to mention a stack of magazines and the TV blasting. I clicked off the TV and started to pick up some of the mess. Found one of Teishia's dirty diapers under the pillow on my couch. That really made me mad. I'm gettin' sick and tired of pickin' up after that girl.

The sound of a sonic boom came from Rashawn's room.

"Turn that stuff *down!*" I shouted. I heard voices. It sounded like someone said "Shhh . . . y'all. It's my momma."

I banged on the door. Somebody turned down the volume—but not enough.

"Rashawn, you got somebody in there with you?"

More voices . . .

Teishia grunted. I looked over at her. She had a funny look on her face. The smell made my nose itch.

Shit . . .

"*Rashawn!*" I knocked again, this time with my fist. I tried the doorknob, but it was locked.

"Rashawn, who's in there?"

Teishia grunted. I looked over my shoulder. Oh, Lord, it was gonna be a big one.

"Just Tiny and Pete, Momma."

Well, that's just great, I said to myself a few minutes later as I wiped Teishia's stinky behind. Pete was OK, but Tiny? "Tiny" was almost seven feet tall, and had four babies by three girls that I knew of. He was a crackhead most of the time. And a thief. He stole the little Walkman my momma gave me for Christmas. He took money outta Bertie's purse once and even took Rashawn's twenty-two, tho' Rashawn had no business keeping a twenty-two in my house in the first place. Tiny was always grinning and bobbing around, gettin' up in my face with "Good mornin', Miz Louis, good evenin', Miz Louis. You all right? You need somethin'? I'll set you up. Get you straight." Negro was always tryin' to give me somethin'. Shoot. He didn't have nothin' I wanted. Well, 'cept maybe for my Walkman he stole. Other than that, Tiny was a lyin', stealin', dirty junkie, and I did not want him in my house.

But tonight was not the night for that either.

I let Tiny stay a little while. I told Rashawn to turn the music down again. He said "Shit." Then he and Tiny and Pete left.

I washed the baby up and put her to sleep in the fold-up playpen. Took me a bath with Calgon and laughed. What does that commercial say? "Calgon . . . take me away."

I sat on the couch and smoked a cigarette. Watched the baby sleep. Heard sirens screaming down Main Street. Lots of noise outside. It sounded like Mardee was havin' another party across the hall. I blindly watched the figures dancing across the TV screen. Ducked down when I thought I heard a gunshot. I drank a Coke and listened to Mardee's party and to the cars going by.

Then I took out my notebook. It's pretty, covered with fabric. A "paisley" print, the saleslady had told me.

I had the pen in my hand—a real ballpoint. It cost me good money at the flea market. It wasn't cheap or nothin'. I took a deep breath, got ready.

My hand didn't move.

What was I gonna say?

You're supposed to have a juicy story to tell on pages like this—a hot love affair like the ones they talk about on the TV, or a long trip to a far-off place.

I looked at the empty page. Then I looked at my good ink pen. I closed the notebook.

You don't write about a COTA bus life in a paisley-fabric-covered notebook.

And you can't write the story of a ninety-nine-cent life with a three-dollar-fifty-cent Parker pen.

A ninety-nine-cent life goes something like this:

At home they call me "Momma." At work, I am "Nita" or "Hey, you!" But my name is Juanita Louis. And *I* like to be called "Juanita."

I live in the projects. They call it low-income housing now. But when I came along ("back in the day" as my kids would say) they called 'em projects. My parents worked hard to move us kids outta there, Daddy worked three jobs and Momma worked two. I remember when we finally moved outta there and into a small two-story frame house off Cleveland Avenue. Mom and Dad were so proud. Nowadays they try to make the projects look like someplace you wanna be, glamorize gunshots and crack-heads. Now, it's called the 'hood.

I got a two-bedroom, but it ain't enough. Bertie and

Teishia (I call her "T") live with me. Teishia's thirteen months old, cute but a handful. Bertie is twenty. She dropped outta high school her junior year and ain't been back. Ain't workin' now either. Collects welfare and has a fine old life watchin' "All My Children" and drinkin' beer and wine coolers.

She usta work checkout at the Big Bear at Town & Country. That girl was always good with numbers—added up the small orders in her head, didn't need to look at the register to make change. Don't know why she quit. Now she tend bar sometime at the Do Drop, says she restin' and wants to be a full-time mother. Funny how *that* works out—I watch T full-time, Bertie is the mother. I work, *she* rests.

She's been gettin' fat here lately. And KC been droppin' by again. I sure hope she ain't pregnant again.

I take one bedroom; my sons, Rashawn and Randy, share the other one. Well, Rashawn does anyway. Randy's away for aggravated assault or something like that. The way the judge told it, he'll be an old man when he come out. He's only twenty-five now.

I send him money for cigarettes and things. Shoot, they gotta buy clothes and bedding and things in there just like they was furnishing an apartment or somethin'. Randy, he's living on snacks now. I guess the food is bad.

Randy says, "Momma, ain't nothin' happenin' in jail, nothin'. All I do is eat, sleep, and try to stay alive."

And talk on the telephone. Randy call here collect so much they turned the phone off 'cause the bill was so high. I tell him not to call me but once every other week, unless he's dyin'. Those collect call charges add up.

Randy doesn't like prison much. I tried to tell him that he wouldn't, but that boy's got a hard head. I hope he'll learn his lesson, but I don't know. Randy was always one to take the shortcuts. 'Course, it'll be a long time before he gets out. By then, Rashawn will be there, too.

Of all my kids, Rashawn at least finished high school. He's got money but no job. He's got clothes, a car, but no job. And people usta knock on my door real late at night. Sometimes wake up the baby. "Zombies" Rashawn calls them. I know what he does and I'm scared. I told him, "The police could come here and take us all away."

I say to Rashawn, "Do your business somewhere else. I don't want that stuff in my house."

He smiles that smile. Dimples, white teeth, like a crocodile grin—a lyin' smile. He says: "OK, Momma, OK. You wanta hold some?"

He shows me a wad of green the size of a cantaloupe.

I say no, now get out.

Rashawn laughs.

He still lives here. But I think he moved his business to an empty double over on Monroe. Once in a while, though, one of those zombies forgets. Come knockin' on my door late at night.

Scare me half to death. I don't open the door. I see them through the peephole: all skinny, gray, and Halloween lookin'. Eyes going every which way, they don't focus on what they're supposed to. They are far away—wherever that pipe is, I guess.

They say, "Rashawn there?"

I lie. I tell them, "Rashawn don't live here no more." I want him to get out for real. He says, "Aw, Mom . . . you trippin'." I think if he don't stop this dealin', I'll be trippin' over his dead behind.

So I'm the only one in the house with a nine to five. I keep three adults in wine and cigarettes, Bertie's Guess? jeans, and these hundred-dollar work boots Randy needs in the "hotel."

I work the second shift at Saint Paul's—they call it Fair-View Medical Center now, but it'll always be Saint Paul's to me. I'm a nurse's aide, which means I clean up the shit and the puke, and do all the other things the nurses too good to do nowadays.

I work from 2:30 to 10:30, but my day starts long before that. I get up at 6:30 to feed T. Bertie, she sleeps till noon. I watch the baby for her till it's time for me to go to work. Seems to me most days, I don't get to see no daylight at all.

I take the bus to work and sometimes I'm thinkin' so hard about things, the driver has to remind me to get off at my stop.

"Hey! Don't you work at the hospital?"

I tell him yes and get off the bus. He shakes his head. Guess he wonders what I'm thinking about that I miss my stop three times a week.

Thinking about things.

At work, it's "Do this!" and "Do that!" all day long. I say, "My name Juan-ita, not Nita." Sometimes I want to smack one of those bitches. Especially the white ones who think I'm a field hand or somethin'. I want to tell them I got news. Slavery was over in 1860 or somethin'. We *all* free now!

But they got lots of sick people, so I stay busy. The time goes fast and before I know anything, my shift is up.

The hospital ain't giving me much. I get $8.50 a hour now. I been there four years. They give the uniforms, but I have to buy white sneakers. We get a discount in the cafeteria, but I don't like the food much so I bring my own.

One thing they give me I appreciate: two fifteen-minute breaks and a lunch hour. For that, I am grateful. I think that by doing that, they gave me my life.

Chapter Two

What happened was this:

I dragged myself into work one afternoon, it was August, I think. One of those hot, hazy, ugly summer days, when it's so muggy the walls sweat.

It was one of those days from hell: T had a cold and fussed all morning, and Bertie wouldn't hardly budge from the bed. I had four loads of clothes to do before work and was tryin' to mix up some ham salad for lunch, too. Add to that Rashawn's loud music and "Montel" and you know what my day was starting off like.

Had to take a later bus, and made it to the fourth floor just in time: I was slipping on my uniform as I punched in. The head nurse, Karen Baronne, Nurse Diesel to you and me, had a bug up her ass that day and was layin' for me.

"Glad you could make it, Louis," she snarled in that way of hers, looking at her watch as if the numbers had turned to diamonds. "We're honored with your presence."

"Yeah, well, whatever," I told her, throwing my stuff

into my compartment, and sliding into my sneakers like I was stealing home. She pulled a stack of charts out, and opened the top one.

"We're down one today. Ruthene claims she's got the flu. You'll have to cover four west by yourself." She grinned at me, looking like the grill on an old Thunderbird with caps. "And Mr. Sayre's got the trots today, so have fun."

"Shit," I said, thinking about the shit I'd have to take off Mr. Sayre. For *real*.

I took a deep breath and headed toward 462. Figured it would be the last deep breath I'd take for a while. Nurse Diesel's voice followed me.

"Better yet, Mr. Sayre can wait a minute. Go to 470 first, Mrs. Berman's daughter might need some help."

I grabbed supplies from the closet as I went by.

"What's she doing in there? Painting the room? Miz Berman ain't no trouble."

"You right about that. Mrs. Berman died just before lunch. Evans-Reagan is about to take the body away. You can help the daughter clear out the room. Dr. Brewster's got four semiwarm ones he wants to send up asap and we need the bed."

I just looked at the bitch. She talked about Miz Berman like she was just a piece of meat. Like she wasn't nobody. Like those four poor souls about to enter this place was nobodies, too.

I put the towels down and walked to Miz Berman's room just in time to see them wheel her out. I patted the white blanket–covered shoulder gently. I had liked Miz Berman, she was OK. She was one of Dr. Guinness's old ladies. He was the cancer doctor, they call it oncology now. I could hear her daughter inside the room, still crying.

Isn't it funny how, even when the flesh is gone, as Reverend Mack says, something's still there? I guess it's the spirit. That old lady, she was a spitfire. Feisty little thing. She took chemo like a champ, went toe to toe with that cancer like Muhammad Ali, pitching and ducking, dodging outta the way. Well, in the end, it got her anyway. But she sure gave old man death a run for his money.

Her daughter sniffled a little while we folded up the gowns and underwear things. She would hand them to me to put in the little suitcase. And even through the clothes and the makeup things, and the fancy tortoise-shell comb and brush, I could feel the fierce snappiness of that old lady. I could feel it through the soft, flannel cloth of a nightgown, the spirit of the woman who sent me to the liquor store a week before for a pint of Wild Turkey and to the carry-out for cigarettes.

"Now, Miz Berman, this is a smoke-free environment," I mocked Nurse Diesel, who was thin-lipped and tight-assed and had no sense of humor. "And alcohol ain't allowed."

Mrs. Berman threw back her tiny head and laughed. Laughed hard. Laughed until she choked, then started coughing. I had to put her oxygen mask back on.

"What will they do, 'arrest me for smoking' as they say in the movies? Throw me out for taking a snort?"

"Aw, Miz Berman . . ." Shoot, I knew a few cigarettes and some liquor wouldn't hurt her. She had the cancer everywhere already.

"Now, Miss Juanita, don't contradict me, just do as I say.

Hell, I'm dying any way you look at it. So why shouldn't I enjoy a nightcap if I want to?"

I sure couldn't think of a reason, so I bought the bourbon and Winstons for her. Late at night, after ten o'clock rounds, that little old lady would pull off her wig, turn on a little tape player her son had brought her, turn out the lights, and sip her bourbon and smoke her cigarettes. I would leave her that way, smoking quietly in the dark, forties swing music playing in the background.

"Good night, Miz Berman."

"Good night, Juanita."

She had some spunk, that old lady.

"What you want to do 'bout these?" I asked the daughter, showing her a tote bag I found at the bottom of the tiny closet. It was filled with paperback books. Mrs. Berman loved to read.

The daughter blew her nose.

"What are they?"

I held up a book.

She snorted, blinked back tears then chuckled, her wet eyes shining in the afternoon sunlight.

"Oh, those." She waved her hand. "I never read *that* kind of stuff. Throw them away . . . no. On second thought, give them to the hospital volunteers." She blew her nose again. "Maybe someone else can get as much pleasure from them as Mother did. They were her one vice."

I decided not to tell Miz Berman's daughter about the bourbon and the cigarettes. And I didn't give the books to the hospital volunteers either.

And, truthfully, I really didn't plan to read them either. I didn't read much then. It all just sort of happened.

By the time me and Miz Berman's daughter finished

clearing out that room, Nurse Diesel started bitching at me for taking so long, one of the other nurses needed help in 424 and there were trays to bus because Dietary Services was running an hour behind. I just stashed those books in my locker and took off down the hall. Spent the rest of the afternoon running to the lab, wiping Mr. Sayre's behind, and moving the comatose patient in 430, among other things. Didn't give that little bag of books much thought until it fell out onto my bunion when I opened my locker before I went down to dinner.

"Shit!" My little Tupperware containers, potato chips, cigarettes, sanitary pads, and those books went everywhere.

"Juanita, you comin'?" asked Patty, one of the girls I worked with. "Leigh's holding the elevator."

Just as she said that, some of the chips spilled onto the floor. There was no way I was going to make Leigh and Patty wait while I picked up all of those crumbs, so I told them to go on. Kicked a book away with my good foot, as I put my dinner back into my tote bag. My toe was killing me. Stuffed the rest of the mess back into the locker and would have closed it, too, except I noticed that damn book over near the nurses' stand where I had just kicked it.

Since I was mad at that book, I picked it up and went to throw it into the trash bin on my way off the floor. But the shiny gold letters on the pink, blue, and silver cover stopped me.

Enchanted Voyage of Love it read. I flipped through the pages, stopped at 361 and tried to read the first two sentences. Didn't know half the words, but I got the point. Rory was kissing that woman in a way that I hadn't been kissed in a long time. It made my toes tingle and left me with a fluttery feeling in the pit of my stomach. I went back to my locker and got the rest of those books.

Took them with me down to the cafeteria, told the girls I had a headache and wanted to be alone. Found me a little table in the corner, and began to look at those books—one by one.

I'd never seen nothin' like them in all my life. On the covers were handsome men with dark hair, muscles on their arms, and fire in their eyes. These men were joined—and I do mean *joined*—at the hip with some young thing whose head was thrown back, her mouth open. They must have been doing it . . . good. Even I felt the heat.

The books had fancy, flowery names like *Passion in Paradise* and *Oceans of Love*. The women who wrote them had fancy names, too: Alexandra Windrush, Priscilla Nottingham.

And the stories themselves? Well, at first I didn't think I could read them. I barely made it through high school. I was five months pregnant with Randy when I wore my cap and gown, so you know I wasn't paying much attention in class. Now that I'm grown, I read when I need to—in order to get my job done, catch a bus, read a label or a sign in the store. Didn't touch newspapers. Watched the news on the TV.

And I never read books. To be honest, I didn't think I could. And I was scared to try.

But the covers grabbed me. They got me to thinking. They made me dream about people long ago. Think about things I couldn't do. Places I would never go.

Lives that I would never live.

I looked at one book with a green and pink cover. I like green and pink. It was called *Love's Prize*.

I opened the cover and read the first page. I almost threw it down. The words were so hard.

Words like "sodden," "uncompromising," "bland," and "adjacent." Lord, I almost gave up.

It took me almost my whole lunch hour to read a few pages. I didn't know what half the words meant.

But I wanted to know.

And I was hooked.

"Juanita? Juanita? You ready to go? It's almost six-thirty, girl. You know, her Witchness will be looking for you. Juanita!"

I couldn't wait until my shift was over. Read a few more pages on the bus ride home, and didn't put the book down again until I fell asleep that night—at four A.M.

On my way to work the next day, I stopped at the drugstore and bought a paperback *Webster's Dictionary* to help with the words I didn't know. And I finished *Love's Prize* three weeks later.

Since then, almost a year ago, I read all the time. I read on the bus to work. I read during breaks and at lunch. And I read at night after I put Teishia to bed, when Bertie and Rashawn go out, and the apartment gets quiet. In fact, now I make Bertie put the baby down by nine o'clock so she's already sleep by the time I get home. That way, all I got to do is take a bath, fix a cold drink, light a ciga-rette, and read. I read all kinds of books, everything I can get my hands on.

When I read, it's like I leave myself, leave my body, and especially leave my life behind and I fly away.

Don't you know I read about a place called Timbuktu? It was a city in Africa, still is, I think. And, back in the day, and I mean a day hundreds of years ago, they had doctors, and famous schools and libraries filled with books. In Africa! Years and years ago. Now, that's a place that I could be.

Or in Russia. Not with the Communists, and with all the mess that's happenin' now, but way back when the czars were in power, and the royalty went around in fancy sleighs, dressed in fur hats and silk underwear.

That's living!

In these books I read, Juanita Louis disappears and becomes a woman who walks the streets of the Forbidden City, or rides out west with Apache warriors. I get to talk with the Pygmy and find out what they know, or dress in designer clothes and run a business and drive a Mercedes-Benz! When I read these stories, I melt away into the woodwork.

And I become somebody.

I leave the projects and the poverty and the sirens and the cursing behind. I dump the cheap wine and the long bus rides and the Kool cigarettes into the trash. I leave it all.

And I have adventures. I have fun and I laugh.

I have a life.

And I am loved.

In the romance novels I read, there's always a man. And soon, he becomes *my* man. He's tall and handsome, smart and brave, and he only has eyes for me. We do it in meadows and on mounds of down-filled pillows, we do it all night, then do it again in the morning. And we enjoy it.

Now, I have done it myself in real life, too. But not like *that*.

Randy's father and I did it in the backseat of his car

when I was sixteen. Randy came along when I was seven-teen. I don't even remember now what it was like.

I married Tyrone Bolte two years later. He had a good job at Timkin, said he'd take care of me and Randy. That's how I got Rashawn. I also got bruises, broken ribs, black eyes, and a miscarriage. Tyrone was the meanest man I ever knew.

Fumbled along for a year or so, married Marvin Wat-son. Pretty man but no job. No life. Just like me. *We* had those two things in common. Oh, yes, and my daughter, Bertie, her real name is Roberta. Marvin and I stayed to-gether for five years, then I woke up one day, looked over at Marvin, and said, "Baby, this party's over, you got to go." I figured if I was a full-grown woman, who had to get up, get dressed, and go to work every day, why was this healthy, full-grown man laying up in my bed with no job? Shit, if I had to work, everyone had to.

Married Rodney Louis on the rebound. It lasted for a year until I rebounded his ass outta my house for carrying on with one of my neighbors upstairs.

You know, I don't remember much about these men. We ate, we drank, we smoked, we slept together, and still, I don't remember much. Except for my children, it's like it never happened.

Not like Lucas, Dominic, Ruark, or Henri. Not like An-dre or Gianni. In my books, the men are dashing, coura-geous, smart—and sexy.

But are there really men like that these days?

Do real people have lives like the ones I read about?

Bertie says I shouldn't read all these books. Says they ain't real: says, "Momma, no one ever had a life like that." She says they're dead anyway, and it's all white folks in those stories. She's wrong about that, and seems like the black folks in these books have great adventures, too.

Rashawn says I'm livin' in a dream world. He says I've turned into a different person since I started reading. Like I'm someone else now.

He just don't know.

Chapter Three

I'd been thinkin' about going away for a while, it wasn't just somethin' that popped into my head. I would see Swee' Pea in my dreams most every night, over and over, carrying that bandanna on a stick. I'd see him crossing oceans and mountains and deserts. Going to China and Egypt. But soon, I didn't see him anymore, I saw myself, taking his place. I saw myself running away instead.

I didn't know where I was goin'. And I didn't know what I was lookin' for. I just knew that I had to get out of *here*. This place, this life, it was choking me. It wasn't enough for me to just *read* about other people and other lives.

I wanted to see it for myself.

I wanted to *live* it for myself.

I couldn't think about what I'd be leavin' behind, 'cause if I had, I wouldn't go. I'd think of a million reasons why I shouldn't.

And I did.

Oh, well, Bertie needs a baby-sitter.

Why? She don't work. She can get up in the morning with her own child. She could get a job, too, except that since she lives with me, and I pay for everything, and do everything *and* keep Teishia, why should she get a job? She's got a fool to take care of all her earthly desires. If I left, Bertie would have to change. She wouldn't have no choice.

Now, would that be a bad thing?

And when I thought about it, hard and clear, without the veil that covered the memories I had of Bertie in a soft, hazy glow. When I ignored the spotty remembrances of the cute, bright-eyed little girl with braids that went every which way, I knew she wouldn't miss me. I had spoiled her. Tried to make things easier for her than they'd been for me. It hadn't worked. She would only miss the things I did for her. Things she would have to start doing for herself.

I heard her talk about me once. She was headed to the mall with one of her friends. Teishia was in the crib taking a nap. Bertie must have thought I was in the bathroom or something.

"You ain't gonna tell your momma you're leavin' Teishia here?" I heard the friend ask.

"She ain't goin' nowhere," Bertie told her. "Don't worry about it."

That wasn't how I wanted to be remembered as a person.

"She ain't goin' nowhere."

And Randy didn't need me. Not really. As far as he was concerned, the only thing I could do for him was send him money and keep the phone on. Well, one money-bags is just as good as another. Randy can get money from Rashawn for cigarettes. Rashawn makes more than me anyway.

Randy was real quiet when I told him I was leaving. The only way I knew he was still there was I could hear him breathing.

"Where you goin', Momma?" he asked me. The static on the line made his voice sound metallic and strange with no emotion, like a robot.

"Wherever I end up, Randy," I answered, knowing how crazy that must have sounded.

Randy didn't say anything else. It was a long-distance call so finally I said good-bye and hung up.

And Rashawn? Well, he's on his own.

Everybody had a life but me. At forty-two, it's about time I had a life, too. Ain't it?

I'll miss little Teishia, she's my heart. But that's all.

Went to say good-bye to my sister, Kay. She does hair at a little beauty shop near downtown. I caught her just as she was finishing a weave. When I told her I was leavin', she just looked at me, narrowed her eyes like she used to do when we was little and I would tattle on her to Momma. She laughed and said, "Girl, you crazy!"

I shrugged my shoulders, picked up a couple of the hair pieces that she was using and fiddled with them.

"Maybe so, but I'm still leavin'."

Kay laughed again.

"Anybody goin' with you? Rashawn? Bertie?"

I shook my head.

"No way."

"You goin' by yoself?"

I nodded. "Uh-huh."

"What, you havin' one of those . . . oh, what they call them things, Doreen?" She hollered over to one of the other girls who was laying on a perm. "That man was on 'Oprah' last week. Whatchu call them things? When people start going crazy when they hit forty?"

"Midlife crisis!" one of the customers yelled back from the shampoo bowl.

Kay snapped her fingers.

"That's it! One of them things." She snatched a piece of hair from me and started to work that woman's head again. "You havin' one of them midlife crises, Juanita? You going to run away and marry a twenty-year-old man, or somethin' like that? Dance on a tabletop?" She laughed, and so did her customer.

But I wasn't laughing.

I said, "Dancing on a tabletop sounds pretty good. Kay, you know I'm gonna go." Kay stopped laughing. Looked at my face. Then put that hairpiece down.

"You for real, ain't you?" she asked me, frowning.

I nodded.

"Honey, you sit here for a minute. I'll be right back." She patted her customer's shoulder, then grabbed me by the arm and pulled me past the shampoo bowls, out the back door, snatching a pack of Newports as she went. The door slammed loud behind us.

"Now what's this all about, Juanita?" she asked sternly in her best big-sister tone. Her dark eyes looked straight into mine.

I told Kay again that I was going away.

"Whatchu mean you going away? What's the matter widchu?"

"Ain't nothin' the matter."

"You OK?" Her eyes widened. "Oh, Lord, you ain't sick, are you?"

Now it was my turn to laugh.

"Naw, KayRita, I ain't sick."

"Hummph." My sister shook her head, smiling. "You sound like you got the blues is all."

"Maybe," I told her. "But I know one thing. I'm tired of this life I been living. It's time for a change."

Kay blew out the smoke.

"Well, we all gets tired, honey. You just gotta deal with it, you know. You don't run away from home, though. Shoot. If everybody that got tired of things ran away, wouldn't nobody be home at all! Now what you gotta do is put them trifling kids out!" Kay rolled her eyes and shook her head while she talked.

"I been after you forever to throw Rashawn out the door. And get Bertie off her butt. It ain't never made no sense to me, Juanita, the way you spoil them kids. Bertie coulda been working at the Big Bear or Kroger."

"Kay, it's time for more than that. *I* got to get outta that place. Leave and start over somewhere else. Doing some-thing else."

"Doing what?" She paused and looked at me. I just looked at her back.

"Somewhere else? Where? Where you gonna go? You don't know no one outside Ohio, except Momma's cousins in Philly, and we ain't even seen them since we was teenagers."

"I know."

"You ain't never been nowhere else, Juanita."

"No shit."

"You ain't never done nothin' else."

"I know that." KayRita was my older sister, but I wasn't backing down off this.

Kay didn't say anything for a second, just smoked her cigarette quietly. The smoke poured out of her nostrils.

"Juanita, you can't just get up and leave home like some kid, runnin' away from your problems. That don't make no kinda sense at all. How you gonna leave here when you don't know where you're going or what you're gonna do when you get there?"

I shrugged my shoulders. It was a good question. But I was beyond worrying about it. "I'm still leavin'," I told her.

Kay looked me hard in the face.

I looked back.

Then she closed her eyes and inhaled deeply on her cigarette. Looked at me again. This time there was a tear in her eye.

Then she said softly, "I think I know how you feel. I wish I could go with you."

After Kay, there wasn't anybody else I needed to talk to. Momma had been dead for five years, and Dad and I weren't close. He had remarried anyway, and was living in Mobile.

I was on my own.

I didn't have much money. Just what was left of my workers' comp check from last year. I didn't tell the kids about that or they woulda had me spend it. I thought maybe I'd run out of money before I got where I'm going, but I could always work. And maybe I'd get lost, but I bought me a map. So I just made up my mind to go where the wind—and the Greyhound—would take me: to the end of the line. To a new life.

Bought two suitcases from the pawnshop.

"Juanita, you need a gold necklace today? I got one just perfect for your slender neck. Just came in." The man behind the counter held out a sparkling strand of gold.

I looked at that man sideways. I ain't never had no slender neck.

"No thanks, not today," I told him, glancing behind the counter. "I need a suitcase, though. Do you have any?"

"Do we have *suitcases*! Are you kidding?" He took me into the back room where at least fifty suitcases stared back at me.

I had to sort through twenty of them before I found the right ones: not too old, not too new, not too big. I felt like Goldilocks.

"You gonna get your VCR out?" the man behind the counter asked me after I paid him.

"No," I said. "Going away for a while."

"Oh, that's nice. Vacation?"

"No," I said, walking out of the door. "New life."

The man called after me.

"New Life? Where's that?"

I'll tell you when I get there, I said to myself.

Wasn't too hard to figure out what to take, I don't have much. Folded-up jeans and T-shirts and socks, some lightweight summer things, some in-betweens. Put sneakers on my feet, left the heels and the Sunday clothes at home. Packed a couple of sweaters, left nail polish and stuff in the bathroom cabinet. If I needed more, I could buy it. Took the Bible my grandma gave me, left all those romance novels behind. I would write my own. Folded up my hospital uniforms and left them on the edge of the bed. Maybe Bertie could use them.

At last I was ready. At eleven in the morning, I had already done more in a few hours than most people do in a whole day. Packed two suitcases, one small cooler, a tote bag, quit my job . . . I felt like Mighty Mouse.

I came out of my bedroom carrying the suitcases and my tote bag, stuffed to the seams. Bertie was just folding up the sofa bed. Teishia was on the floor, playing with her toes. Bertie looked pissed.

"Momma, where were you? I had to get up at eight-thirty with T this mornin'." Noticing the suitcases for the first time, she asked, "Where you going?"

"Going away for a while," I replied. (In my "old" life, I would have used "I said." In my new life, however, I "replied.")

"Goin' where?" asked Rashawn, who came out of the bedroom, yawning and scratching. "Momma, you didn't tell nobody you was goin' nowhere."

"That's 'cause I'm forty-some years old," I told him as I knelt down to give T a kiss. "I don't have to tell anybody anything."

Rashawn frowned.

"How long you be gone?"

"Don't know yet."

"Momma, you trippin'!" exclaimed Rashawn. His deep voice rumbled like thunder in the small living room. "What's up widchu?"

"What you mean you don't know?" screeched Bertie. "What about your job at the hospital? Who's gonna keep Teishia for me?"

I kissed little Teishia again and set her, squirming, back onto the floor.

"In the first place, Bertie, I quit the hospital this morning. In the second place, you don't have a job or anything else to do. You can keep Teishia yourself."

I felt as if I had blurted out a complicated math problem. I couldn't help but grin. Of course, Bertie didn't think much of my idea.

"But Momma! I think I'm pregnant again! What am I gonna do? I need my rest!" she wailed, tears streaming down her face. "I'm gonna need some money . . ."

"Momma, what's wrong widchu? You gone crazy?" Rashawn's face was dark like a thunderstorm about to break. Now he reminded me of his father—the way Tyrone looked just before he broke my jaw. Once, a long time ago, I would have been scared. Now, I simply did not give a damn.

"No, Rashawn, I'm not crazy. Bertie, you'll just have to get along. You're young, you can work. They always need aides at the hospital."

"I can't believe you! Just leavin' us like that," Rashawn bellowed. "I can't believe it."

"Well, believe it," I shot back. He acted like he and Bertie were ten years old!

"You got shit for brains?" he roared at me. "You read them books, think you a white woman or somethin'? Think you just gonna dance outta here and into a new life? Like *you* got somethin' somebody wants?" He got up in my face so close I could see the flecks of gold in his eyes. Mean, nasty eyes. Like his daddy's. "Well, here's the news, Momma, and it's up to the minute. This is *real* life. And in real life, you ain't nothin'."

I slapped him. Hard. All six feet, two inches and one

hundred ninety pounds of him stumbled back toward the couch.

Bertie gasped. Looked at me like I was crazy. Maybe I was.

"I'm your momma. Don't you ever talk to me like that! I may not be much to *you*, but to myself, I'm enough."

Rashawn didn't say anything. Just looked at me like he hated my guts.

"Now you both listen to me, and you listen good. And you can pass this on to Randy, too. All your life I have taken care of you, most of the times by myself, too. I paid the rent, the food, everything! I paid for Teishia, and I work my fingers to the bone for y'all, for Teishia. And what have I got to show for it? I'll tell you: I ain't got shit! Unless you count grown children who expect me to wait on them hand and foot and give them money. You all will use me until you use me up and there's nothing left. Well, I'm through with that. I'm taking the little bit of me I got left and gettin' outta here. You can take care of yourselves."

"But Momma! Where you goin'?" whined Bertie. "When will you be back?"

"Momma? Momma?"

I closed the door behind me. "I don't know where I'm goin' or when I'll return," I told them in my new voice using my new words. I am a new woman now. And I must use new language. "I'll call you."

How could I answer their questions? Heroines who have great adventures don't have time limits and they don't have . . . what they call them things? Agendas. They don't have no agendas. They take what fate hands out. They go where the wind blows.

My tote bag was full but not with novels. I was leaving them at home. I had packed spiral notebooks and pen re-fills instead.

I was going to write about my own great adventure.

And I wasn't going to do it with no ninety-nine-cent pen either.

Chapter Four

OK, you're leaving home. Got your bags packed, food in the cooler, cash money in your pocket. All ready to go.

Where?

It's hard to know where to go when you haven't been anywhere.

Years ago, when my sister and brother and I were kids, my momma took us on the bus to Cleveland when our grandfather died. Another time, we visited some great-aunts or someone in Akron. I think Momma sent me and Kay alone, but I was real little then and I don't remember much. We drove to Springfield once for a Memorial Day picnic when I was about twelve. I remember that it was cool that day, and that it rained.

That's it.

That's all of my travel experience.

So when I got to the bus station, it was time to make a decision. I found a spot not too far from the ticket counter, sat down, and looked at the road atlas that I bought at the bookstore. Where was I goin', exactly? East? West? North? South?

To the east were the big cities—Philadelphia, D.C., New York. They didn't really appeal to me. I had cousins in Philadelphia, but I hadn't seen them in years. Besides, cities meant more noise and tall buildings, police and projects, gunfire and poverty.

I could stay home and see all that.

To the north were places like Cleveland and Detroit. More of the same old stuff.

Minneapolis? Canada? Didn't pay much attention to geography when I was a kid. I never realized there was so much up north. Thought about it for a minute, but changed my mind. Well, I didn't have room for a coat anyway. Maybe I could go to Quebec and Montreal on my way back. If I came back.

The South? Atlanta, Memphis, Louisville, New Orleans, the Great Smokies, and tall pines of Georgia. My grandmother was born in northern Georgia. She told us stories about it: rolling hills, forests thick with those huge Georgia pine trees, hot, lazy summers. That sounded nice. I'd heard that Atlanta was a nice city, black folks were doing things down there. My finger slid over to Pensacola and down toward Naples. Florida sounded OK, too. Saw myself walking along a sandy beach in a bikini. Had to laugh out loud at that thought.

" 'Scuse me!" Some kid tripped over my feet. "I'm sorry."

"That's all right." I moved my size nines out of the way, scooted the suitcases closer to my seat. Glanced over at the ticket counter, which was empty now.

Buses leaving for Atlanta, Chattanooga, Cleveland, and New York City in the next hour. One bus headed for Cincinnati any minute, one going to Indianapolis at four. And one headed west through St. Louis to Denver, Colorado.

Colorado. I flipped through the atlas till I found it. West. I had forgotten to look there.

There aren't many cities after St. Louis. Not unless you look to California, or south to Texas. The states are big, boxy-looking things with names like Nebraska, South Dakota, and Wyoming. The mountain ranges crisscross the land, and dotted lines marked Indian reservations and parks here and there. Then on to California, and the ocean.

Put my finger on Columbus, Ohio, traced a line straight through to Denver, then up to those mountains I had seen. Up through Wyoming, and on to a state I had forgotten existed.

I gathered up my stuff and shuffled over to the counter.

"Ma'am?"

"One way to Butte, Montana, please."

The man whistled. Punched keys on the machine.

"Boy, that's a long way. Most people stop at St. Louis, or go all the way to L.A. You got family in Butte?" He told me the cost of the ticket.

"Nope," I answered, digging in my wallet. "Just going to see."

He counted out my change.

"Ten, thirty-five, forty. Going to see what?"

I almost felt silly when I answered him, but in truth, I was serious.

"Whatever's there."

The man looked at me kinda funny when he handed me my ticket. He probably thought I was crazy, let out of the state hospital this morning. And guess what?

I didn't care. Heroines can't get tied up with stuff like that. We're too busy living our exciting lives.

The bus wasn't real crowded, so I got to spread out over two seats instead of one. Situated myself against the window, and pulled out my pillow. Saw a lot of other folks doing the same thing.

There were a few people who looked like they had their whole lives with them: suitcases about to bust, shopping bags, tote bags with shoes falling out all over the place, plastic bags. Other folk don't have anything with them but a purse, or just hands in their pockets. Does that mean they just pack light? Or they don't have much of a life to pack?

The older ladies always got to me. Packed to the gills, they carried suitcase after suitcase, boxes, grocery sacks, faded tote bags—all kinds of things. And you know what was sad about that? Their lives were in those suitcases, years and years of husbands and children, grandchildren, little jobs that didn't add up to much even when they were put together, church dinners and Social Security and chump change. I knew about lives like that.

If I wasn't getting out of this place, I would be sixty-some years old before long, with my whole life packed in a brown paper grocery sack.

Some kids, teenagers, pushed through the bus to the back with half-shaved heads hooked up to CD players, black combat boots, and half-empty army surplus duffel bags, earrings in their ears, eyebrows, noses, and navels. I could hear somebody screaming in the background—those headphones really didn't work too good. Those kids would be deaf before they're twenty-five.

They were too young to have much in their bags, hadn't lived long enough to have any real baggage. The kind that life leaves you with.

And me?

Well, I had left most of mine at home. And one of the blue suitcases I bought was half empty. I was saving space for whatever my new life would bring. Or maybe, I thought then, I'd bring it back empty again. Who knew what would happen?

As the bus pulled away, most of the folks seemed to be ready to take a nap. Not me. I pulled out a notebook and my pen. It was time to write about the beginning of my adventure.

I sat there for a while, counting red cars on the freeway, reading the signs and thinking how they'd put a McDonald's at every exit now, and wondering how to start. I flipped through the blank pages of the book and looked at the herds of cows I saw in the fields.

I guess I was procrastinating. (A new word I had learned.) I wanted to start writing but I was arguing with myself. What do I tell? How do I begin? Do I start with the time I stepped into this bus? Or do I start at the beginning? The very beginning. The day I was born, or the first real memory I had. Read somewhere that you can't go nowhere unless you know where you've been. But God knows I hated to waste good paper on that mess. Yet I still thought long and hard about it. If I wrote it down, then I could read it over and over and remember. So that I wouldn't make all those same mistakes again. I started to write.

I put it all down, I didn't leave anything out. I told about my previous life: when I was little and what it was like growing up, about my husbands, Randy's father, Teishia, and my job. About what it was like to live in a gray world, like when TV was only black and white.

My parents were good people. They worked hard and tried to help us kids along as best they could. Daddy grew up on the tail end of the depression. Just the idea of being hungry and being poor scared him to death. He could squeeze the life out of a dime. He worked all the time—two jobs, three jobs—just to make sure that we kids had enough to eat and that the lights stayed on. There wasn't a job around that Daddy didn't like. He kept his money in the mattress—now, how old-fashioned is that? He didn't believe in throwing nothing out; we never had garbage. If Mom made a pot of beans, we ate them till the sight of 'em made us sick.

Dad was a decent man, but his fear of being poor and taking handouts took away his laughter. He never smiled. Least not as far as I can remember. And when you looked in Daddy's eyes, you saw desperation and worry, even when the light bill was paid and Mom's pantry was full. Daddy was always afraid. Always.

Mom smiled more but worked just as hard. Worked herself half to death, I think. She raised three kids and kept a garden the size of Indiana after we moved into the house over on 11th Avenue. She served in the Nurses' Corps at Mount Ararat Baptist—no Sunday ever started without her. She worked in the cafeteria at Central High School and did a little tailoring on the side. Mom could do anything with a needle and thread. She did it all so that we could have more, so that my sister, brother, and I could *be* more. KayRita did all right. She went to beauty school, and started doing hair right out of high school. But after that, everything went wrong. My brother died young. And I got pregnant in the eleventh grade.

I remember when I told my momma that I was having a baby. I was young, stupid, and thought I was cute. Had the nerve to stick my chin out at Mom and tell her what my plans were. How grown-up I thought I was. I told her all about how I could take care of myself and the baby and didn't need nobody to tell me what to do.

What a stupid bitch I was then.

I remember thinking that Mom's whole face changed that day. That, somehow, her complexion lost its luster, and her dark brown eyes, which my granddaughter Teishia has inherited, weren't as bright anymore. But back then, I thought I was just imagining things.

But I wasn't. Twenty-some years later, I know what happened to my momma. Because the same thing happened to me when *my* daughter told me she was pregnant. It was the hope that went out of my momma's face: the hope she had that I would finish school, and maybe have a chance to live a decent life. A life better than the one she had. Well, it died when I told her about the baby. And I never saw hope in Mom's eyes again as long as she lived.

She never told nobody about that lump she found. Not even Kay, who was her favorite child. Mom never told no one until the damn thing was so big that it had spread its poison all through her skinny body, and there wasn't hardly nothing left.

I put my pen down.

I looked out the window, but the other cars were

blurry, and I couldn't see much besides colors through my tears.

Hope was something that my momma lost and never got back.

I had lost it, too.

But now I was going to try to get it back.

When I was twenty-one years old I was married to Tyrone Bolte, who worked double shifts at Timkin. He had fistfuls of money, and spent it like most folks drink water. I remember we went and bought new furniture, and Tyrone paid cash money for it—laid out four one-hundred-dollar bills on the store counter. That salesman's jaw like to drop to the ground! It was the first and last time (so far) in my life that I had a car that ran steady.

But Tyrone had demons on his back, and when they got a good grip around his neck, he'd do whatever he had to do to shake them off. I never knew what it was in his life that tortured him so. But when it did? Tyrone turned into a devil like you've never seen.

He drank like a sailor, tore up most of the new furniture we'd bought, and beat the shit out of me. And you never knew when he would start up, or what would set him off. Seems like every day of those three years I spent with Tyrone I walked on eggshells and talked in a whisper.

When Rashawn was nine months old, I was five months pregnant, and Tyrone got drunk and mad at me for buying a bedspread at Kmart on sale. When he got finished with me, the bedspread was cut up so bad I couldn't return it, and I wasn't pregnant no more. I was a few teeth short, too. I told the policeman he was just a little upset, and I lay down with that man in the same bed that night.

I must have been crazy or stupid. Or both. Now that I think about it, I'm lucky to be alive. Last thing I heard, Tyrone is serving fifteen to life. He killed his second wife because she wanted to sell Avon.

I tell about the hospital and all the people I met there—most of the ones I really helped died, but there's no way around that when you work the cancer floor. The nurses say you get used to it, but I don't see how. You get close to those people, and watch them fight death, and suffer. And you don't want 'em to suffer, but you got to hand it to them when they fight back at death just to grab a few more moments of daylight. I write about old Mrs. Berman and cigarettes and her liquor, and her gift of books, and the zombies who knocked on my door late at night looking for Rashawn.

"*Hey!* Rashawn there? I need to get wid him, you know. Huh? Whatchu mean he ain't live here? Look, you don't understand, bitch. I need to get wid him, you know what I mean?"

I write about my apartment and the street where I live, and I even tell about the little man at the pawnshop who wanted to know where "New Life" was. I talk about the long days, my off days, the ones before I began to read, before I knew there was a whole other world. I talk about the days when my life was wrapped up in talk shows and soaps, and measured from one commercial to the next. Now, that is no life at all.

Bertie was my running buddy in those days, when I should have been making her go to work or school; when she should have been meeting other young people who were doing things with their lives. Instead, we both sat like lumps on the couch, smoking, patting Teishia, and discussing Erica Caine's plans and the people in Jerry Springer's audience. I let the soaps and the talk shows go after I started reading. I didn't care anymore. All I could think of was living a life of my own that would be worth mentioning somewhere. Even a footnote life was better than the one I had.

I wanted that to change.

I tell it all, all my past life. I try not to leave anything out, try to tell the good parts and the bad parts. 'Course, there's more bad than good, and more "just OK" than anything else. Then I draw a thick, red line.

Past this red line, no words about the past life will ever go. It is the present and what is to come that will fill these pages. No wish I hads or I shouldas. Only "I did."

I remember my grandmother and grandfather talking over dinner once, long ago when I was a child. Grand-daddy asked Grandma if anything had happened at a meeting she had attended. I remember what she said.

"Nothing to write home about."

I remember wondering what she meant by that. In my child's mind, I saw my grandmother sitting there at her meeting, pulling out a little piece of paper and a pencil, and an envelope, then changing her mind and putting it all away again.

Now, of course, I know what she meant.

Nothing of value came out of her meeting.

I want a life worth writing home about.

Chapter Five

I was only a few hours away from home, but it seemed like I was traveling in a foreign country.

I guess I had forgotten that Ohio was mostly a farming state. There were fields of green corn and golden wheat as far as I could see. Wide-open spaces filled with cows, or rocky, funny-shaped hills spotted with sheep that didn't look anything like the little lamb that Mary had. Their fleece was gray and grimy. Silos stuck out here and there, and sometimes I'd see a man sitting up on a tractor, working straight lines into the earth.

The space, the openness was strange to me. Houses and towns were miles apart, and seemed to like it that way. Even the garages were far from the homes, as if the people who lived there don't want the car too close. White clothes flapped in the breeze on clotheslines, now that was kinda pretty. I hadn't seen that in a while. There was no use drying clothes outside where I lived. The last time one of my neighbors did that, all her clothes were stolen.

I don't know, I don't think the air was that fresh anyway. Not like out here.

The bus turned onto another highway, and the scenery changed a little. The road wound back and forth through the quietest, greenest land I had ever seen. Here there were no barns, silos, or houses. Just green, as far as the eye could see. Tall, funny-looking trees, all bunched together. There wasn't much sound either.

I opened the window. I knew that I wasn't supposed to (the AC was on) but that manufactured air was giving me a headache. I was raised by a woman from central Georgia. My momma didn't believe in air-conditioning. If it was four thousand degrees outside, Momma would say, "It's a little warm." I poked my head out the window and took a deep breath of Ohio country air and diesel fumes.

I heard a hawk screeching but nothing else. Inside, the bus was quiet, too. I guess everyone else was either asleep or in a daze like I was. We went along like this for miles with no passing cars, no houses in sight.

The bus slowed to a crawl, and began to climb up a little hill. The engine whined a little as if it didn't want to go any farther. The passengers murmured among themselves, necks craning as they tried to see what was going on. Then, suddenly, up over the ridge, I saw them.

Over the loudspeaker, the driver spoke: "Sorry for the delay, folks, but, in case you didn't know, this is Amish country and they've got the road blocked off up ahead. Looks like a meeting of some kind . . . no, sorry. A funeral. They're probably walking to the cemetery over the next hill. They'll turn off here shortly, and then we'll be on our way in a few moments."

Now, you know I'm nosy. I practically pushed my whole

body out that window. I wanted to get a good look so I could write it all down. I'd never seen anything like this. You know, there were no Amish people in my neighborhood.

There were lots of them, all walking quietly, or riding in black, horse-drawn buggies, or in wagons. They wore gray or black, the women's heads were covered with bonnets, the men wore wide-brimmed black or straw hats and had long beards. There was no talking among them, no noise. I could barely hear the sound of their feet stepping on the roughly paved road. Even the children, and there were lots of them, were silent.

The lead buggy, which I just barely caught a glimpse of, carried a small, wooden coffin, and I felt my chest tighten. This was the funeral of a little child. I thought of Teishia and tears came to my eyes. There ain't nothin' more sad than one of those tiny, little caskets. Nothin'.

The bus stayed a respectful distance behind the funeral procession, moving slowly until the people began to move onto a side road that led around a bend. Then as the last of the group begins to make the turn, the bus picked up a little speed, and moved past.

Most of the people didn't even look up, as if they were trying to ignore us. The roar of the bus engine didn't appear to disturb their thoughts, the metallic smell of the diesel fuel wasn't interfering with the sweet air they were used to breathing. Maybe they figured if they didn't see us, we didn't exist and couldn't threaten their way of living. Others, especially some of the younger boys, looked over real quick, and then looked back. Their expressions were curious but not sad. The women didn't look up at all.

Except for one.

I caught a glimpse of her as we rolled past. She glanced up at the bus and looked at me. I remember being surprised to see a face that was puffy and eyes that were red. I knew I was seeing a heart that had been broken. I wondered if she was the child's mother. The bus roared by and the woman's face was hidden by a blast of gray smoke.

But I never forgot her or her sadness. I wrote it down. I thought about that woman's face for a long time. I still think about her even now, many days later and a thousand miles away.

I knew what that kind of sadness was about.

It's hard to put into words, hard to explain to other people. It's everywhere and it can surround you like the air you breathe. But it's hard to *see*.

After Tyrone Bolte kicked me and I wasn't pregnant anymore, the funeral home put my baby in a little, tiny box and took her away. I cried until I couldn't cry anymore. I didn't eat for a week. And I put flowers on the marker that's in the cemetery where they buried her. I didn't have any money of my own to put a headstone there. So I just kept putting flowers on that little marker, and whispered the little girl's name to myself so that no one else could hear.

Tyrone was really sorry about the baby. He cried and begged me to forgive him and take him back. Ignorant as I was, I did take him back. But I never forgave him.

And I never told him where that baby was buried, or what I named her. I figured that she didn't need to be visited by the man who killed her.

I just kept her life and her death to myself since I was the only person who ever really knew her anyway.

I found that I was becoming claustrophobic. In reverse. I was used to living in a tiny, Cracker Jack–sized apartment, with four families above, four families below, and two on either side. Big families, lots of people: Mardee in 1026 had four kids, two of her daughters had babies, her father lived there and her son's girlfriend and *their* baby. Ten people. And she only had three bedrooms. I had two. I guess I was lucky—just me, Bertie, Rashawn (and Randy, when he was there), and Teishia.

But out here, the farms are minutes not seconds apart. And they appear one at a time, not in bunches. I spied one lonely, white farmhouse with green shutters and didn't see the next one for a whole minute, sometimes two. I couldn't get used to that. Mile after mile and not one person in sight—horses, cows, even buffalo, but no people. Miles of gold and green. Plants. Weeds. Rocks.

No people.

It gave me the shakes just like my sister used to get when she rode the elevator. Kay said she felt trapped, crazy, and panicked, and that she couldn't breathe.

And there were no *sounds*. Where were the sirens that I got so used to that they put me to sleep? What about the slamming of doors and the sound of liquored voices raised in anger, screaming babies, desperate knocking at my door?

Now there is only the sound of grass growing, the piercing screech of a hawk, the roar of an eighteen-wheeler's engine zooming by in the passing lane. It makes me a little nervous, this kind of quiet. It makes me think too much, to remember what I'd like to forget. Maybe I'm not ready for big, open spaces. City noises were a great mask. You could always say it's too loud to think, too hectic to wonder about universal truths, too dangerous to remember something pleasant or painful. You can use the noise as an excuse for not opening your mind. You can hide behind the sound of gunshots and car horns. And you can starve your soul because that's what it really lives on: thinking, remembering, reflecting.

Ohio and Indiana weren't bad. I'm familiar with the Midwest. I know what it's supposed to be like, even though I've never really been out of the city. Missouri was OK, too, still familiar.

But Kansas was different. Flatter than Nurse Diesel's behind, miles and miles of wheat blowing in the breeze, no people, no buildings in sight most of the time. Empty, flat land. Haunted, almost. I tried to ignore it. I went to sleep. Hoping that when I woke up, we'd be in a city, where I would feel safe.

But when the sun rose again, I saw the mountains, evergreen forests stretched out to forever, and wondered if I was making a mistake. Wanted to catch the next bus back to Columbus, Ohio, and go into my little apartment, and my little room, close the door and hide.

Flat, green-and-gold fields I can live with. A black-and-white life I can live with.

But mountains? I had no experience with mountains. I didn't know any snowcapped peaks personally, and the sight of the pine forests, spread out for miles around, made my knees weak.

Everything here is huge, spread out, and empty. There are more elk than people, more eagles than cars. I'm not used to so much.

Now I was really afraid. I thought that I had made a big mistake.

What was I doing here?

I panicked. I thought, "I'm not ready for this. Maybe I should head for Los Angeles after all. And hide. In a closet."

Instead of visiting this tiny dot on the map. A little place I just picked on a whim because it had a cute name, and I figured it would be as good a place as any to begin. It's west of Missoula, south of Thompson Falls, small letters near the junction of Interstate 90 North and Route 135 on the map, near the Idaho border and south of Kootenai National Forest. Out in the sticks. Not far from the middle of nowhere.

A town called Paper Moon. I picked it because Teishia giggled when I played the Natalie Cole version of the song. Other than that, I didn't know why I was going there, other than I wanted to go somewhere different from the places I had been. (Since I hadn't been anywhere, that was pretty easy.)

And from what I could tell, little Paper Moon, Montana, population one thousand, situated at the base of a mountain, not far from Lake Arcadia, was about as far from where I'm from as you could get.

I was afraid of open plains, mountains, forests, lakes, and wildlife.

And I was headed to Montana.

I should have had my head examined.

So there I was sitting in a coffee shop in Butte, eating the best pot roast I ever had, and studying my little road atlas. Wondering how in the world I was ever going to get to Paper Moon, Montana. It was over two hundred miles away. Going there had seemed like a good idea at the time, but now that I really thought about it, it made no sense at all. Hitching a ride on the space shuttle might

-year-old grandmother who's running away from
see the world? I've left a pregnant, unemployed
r, a drug-dealing son, and another son who's in
? That I've quit my job, and I have a little less than
housand dollars to my name? *And* I've set out to find
ortune? To have a great adventure and see things I've
er seen before? That I'm becoming a new person? Do
u tell *that* to people you don't know but who want to
now who you *really* are?

I couldn't tell her *that*! She'd think I was some kind of
nut! Like I walked away from a padded cell yesterday. It
was the truth, but when I put it into sentences it sounded
crazy! And stupid!

The next thing I knew, one side of me was arguing with
the other.

"You can't be goin' around telling some strange white
woman about your business, Juanita! What's wrong with
you?"

The other voice said, "Negro, *please* ... Like you're
holdin' secrets for the FBI? What could possibly be goin'
on in your $3.50 life that needs to be locked up in a vault?
Tell that woman anything you want!"

I made up my mind to do just that but I didn't get the
chance to do it right then. Peaches had moved on with
the conversation, and so I ended up listening instead, between bites of pot roast, mashed potatoes, and green
beans. She told me all about herself, between long drags
on her Viceroys and deep gulps of black coffee.

She was twenty-eight, lived in Cheyenne, and owned
her own eighteen-wheel tractor trailer, hauling for some
of the large discount retailers in this part of the country.
She was one of very few female truckers working in the

have been easier for me than catching a ride to northwest
Montana. Maybe I should have picked somewhere else.
And there was another thing.

In case you didn't know, there aren't many black folks
in this part of the country. Funny, I never thought of that
when I decided to take this trip—that I might be going
places where black folks didn't live, where black folks
might not even be welcome. But since Denver, I hadn't
seen one brown face. And judging by the hostess's expression when she served my meal, the folks in Butte hadn't
seen one either.

The hostess stared at me for a few seconds before saying "Good morning" and inviting me to seat myself. Some
of the patrons actually turned a little on their stools and
studied me with blank but curious expressions. And the
waitress almost spilled my Coke in my lap.

There wasn't any hostility. And I didn't think the manager would ask me to leave or anything. But I could just
tell that they didn't see people like me very often. And
from the looks on their faces, they weren't sure yet if that
was bad or good.

So I sat in the little booth, chewed on the roast beef,
and wondered whether I should scrap my trip to Paper
Moon and head for Seattle instead. I almost changed my
mind. It's a good thing I met Peaches when I did.

"You're not from around here."

Startled, I looked up and found a broad-faced young
woman smiling at me and fixing to sit down. I had seen
her when I first came in here, but from the back I had
thought she was a man with her stocky, fireplug-like build,
square jaw, and dirty blond hair tucked under a Reds cap.

Her voice was hoarse and a little rough to listen to, a serious smoker's voice but not unpleasant, and from under the brim of the cap, her blue eyes twinkled at me.

"What tipped you off?" I asked her, sarcastically.

"The scarlet-and-gray sweatshirt," she answered guilelessly. I could tell my sarcasm would be wasted on her. "No Buckeyes up this way. Mostly U of M brown and yellow." She shrugged her shoulders a bit. "Yeah, the air-conditioning is going full tilt in here."

She moved to sit down, but my two dusty, beat-up suitcases were in her way. It didn't matter. She just scooted them over and made herself right at home in my life. "Looks like you're running away from home."

"Yeah, sorta," I said, amazed at her boldness. She didn't know me from Adam.

But there was something about her that I liked right away. She was one of those real-deal, open people. Guileless. (Another one of my new words.) She didn't look like her but this girl was a lot like my sister, KayRita. She didn't know any strangers.

"You go, girl. Sometimes you gotta do that. Show 'em who's boss. Keeps 'em from taking you for granted at home." She took a long, deep drink from the huge travel coffee mug she was carrying. "Ernie's Truck Stop 'n' Suds" it said in green letters.

"Ah, well, I . . ." I couldn't think of anything to say. Not that it mattered. She was on to her next sentence.

"Mind if I join you? Seeing as you're a fellow Buckeye." Nice of her to ask. "Sorry to be so blunt, but I'm from Middletown, myself. Don't see many folks from Ohio out here. Ohioans don't usually pass through Montana on their way West. They fly over it, and go directly to L.A." She plopped

her ample behind onto the N[...] and held out a square h[...] such a rush. I'm Penelop[...] want to lose a few teeth ca[...] rette. The smoke came out [...] cloud like it did from Mount S[...] saw a while ago when it blew its t[...]

"I'm Juanita Louis, nice to meet yo[...]

She exhaled again and took her ha[...] round head, freckles, and a huge, Kool-Aid[...] spilled everywhere, falling over her shoulde[...] fall of hair down to her waist.

"Where you from?"

"Columbus."

"Ahh . . . the capital." She nodded, taking another s[...] of her coffee. "Yeah, we used to go there for the fair. Biggest damn fair in the country, isn't it? Mom and Dad loved the corn dogs and the ices. I'd stuff myself with Belgian waffles, onion rings, and cotton candy till I puked. It was *great*. Boy, do I get homesick!"

I was getting sick myself, but I took a sip of Coke instead.

"Don't you get back there much?" I asked her.

Peaches shook her head. Her hair went every which way.

"No reason to. Dad left when I was thirteen and Mom's been dead for years. I have a sister but . . ." She lit a cigarette and inhaled deeply. She changed the subject. " 'Sides, I live in Wyoming and all of my routes are west and north. What brings you out here? Butte isn't exactly a hot spot. You passing through?"

"I . . ." I paused for a few seconds. I had to stop and think. Just how much of your business do you tell to a complete stranger? And what should I say anyway? I'm a

Northwest, and her "handle" for the CB was "Orchard Honey," referring to her nickname of "Peaches," a childhood nickname given her by her mother, whom she had loved a lot.

"My mom was a sweet woman, she had class and manners. Not like me." Peaches paused and took this opportunity to belch loudly. Then she grinned, her smile wide and bright like a child's and just as full of mischief. Then she belched again. "Love that Coke!"

I had to giggle.

"Mom was a large woman, close to three hundred pounds, but she had a tiny little voice, all whispery, like the way Marilyn Monroe sounds in movies." Peaches stopped for a moment as if she was trying to remember something. "She was born in a little spot down in Randolph County, West Virginia, no running water, no toilets, you know, real hillbilly life. Her family never had money, they just scratched out a living. Mom never even wore shoes much until she married my dad and moved to Ohio. But you know, my mother had more style and honest love for people than anyone I ever knew. She tried to teach that to my sister and me."

I thought that Peaches's mom sounded a lot like my mom.

"Do you get to see your family much?" I asked, thinking for a moment about my own sister, so far away, and my mother, now long gone. "Oh, sorry," I said. "I asked you that before."

"That's OK. Not much family left," Peaches said matter-of-factly. "After Dad ran off, Mom got the sugar so bad . . ." She stopped and lit a cigarette, but didn't say anything.

"Just you and your sister, huh?" I tried to finish the

thought for her. I knew how she felt. KayRita and I were the only ones left in our family. And even though I was a grandmother, and closer to fifty than to twenty, there was something a little lonely about there being just the two of us left. Without Mom and Daddy around, without our brother Jerome, the world was cold and empty and scary— the memories were the only things we had—and Kay and I were the only ones left who remembered them. I shivered a little. I tried not to think of what life would be like if I didn't have my sister.

"Well, yes," Peaches agreed slowly, blowing a thick cloud of smoke into the air. "But we don't get along. She doesn't approve of my . . . my . . ." She chuckled. There was something off-center or offbeat about that chuckle. Like an orange that was tart instead of sweet, or a Coca-Cola that had gone flat. Peaches smiled wickedly.

"She doesn't approve of my 'lifestyle choice,'" she said sarcastically, pronouncing each word as if I would give her a prize for the number of syllables they had.

At first I didn't get it. Let me say that again. I got it, but I had to think about it a little.

Then I felt dumb.

When I first started reading, and then really noticing the world around me, I got real embarrassed. The books seemed to shine a light on just how ignorant and unaware I was. There were all kinds of things going on in the world that I just had no idea about. Situations I had never heard of, history that I had not known about. Places I'd never see.

I felt stupid all of a sudden. Wanted to hide myself, thinking that somehow my ignorance showed on my face, like one of those signs they have at football games that tell you where the Coke and popcorn are sold, and what the score is. Only this one said "Juanita don't know shit."

Then I put that feeling sorry for myself stuff aside and read even more. I tried to read the hard-core stuff like *Moby Dick* (don't know why, but I just couldn't get into that whale), Edgar Allan Poe (he made me more sad than scared), and the Brontë sisters (something different about those girls, I'll tell you that). The stuff between the lines got easier to understand as the words *on* the lines did.

But just as I thought I had it, just as I thought I knew language and what words meant, even when they had lots of meanings in the dictionary, the fashionable words came in.

And I got ignorant again.

People weren't experts on things, they were "gurus."

A person with a hearing aid became "auditorially challenged" and all around me restaurants were turning into "bistros" serving chicken from a "free range."

And as I found with Peaches, a decision about who to love had turned into a "lifestyle choice."

It was so complicated!

The "life's choice" that had put her and her sister at loggerheads was not the vagabond life of the trucker but the fact that Peaches was gay. Her sister was one of those tight-assed Bible-belt types who would disapprove of chewing gum if given half a chance. She had told Peaches she would die in agony and burn in hell forever. Peaches's reply was classic: If heaven was full of people like her sister, then hell would definitely be the way to go. I guess that remark separated them for good.

"I told her, 'You know what, Lorene? Your ass is so tight

that you'd have to get someone to give you mouth-to-mouth just to open it up a little so that you could use the can once in a while!' "

I laughed so hard that I choked on my water.

I was on dessert—banana cream pie—when she finished telling her story and finally got around to asking me where I was headed. We'd been talking for almost an hour and I guess we'd talked about everything but that.

"Paper Moon."

Peaches's blue eyes widened and she set her coffee cup down.

"Paper Moon? Montana?" She stared at me with her mouth open.

I nodded.

"Why on earth would you want to go there? It's in the middle of nowhere. The only reason I even know about it is that I drive that way once a month or so, on my route to Canada. Humph . . . little Paper Moon . . . I haven't been there in a while."

"I thought I'd take the bus to Missoula, then on to Redfish," I told Peaches. "I'd probably have to spend the night there and try to meet up with someone who's going north. Maybe one of the students at. . . ." I studied the little atlas. "West Montana Valley State College. The bus driver says that the students are always going somewhere on the weekends, and by then it'll be Friday."

"Don't bother, I can take you there," Peaches said with finality. "No use you going through all of that. That's almost like hitchhiking. And there are a lot of sick puppies out there, let me tell you. Besides, there aren't many students at Valley State for summer term anyway. It might be tough to get a ride."

"Oh, no," I told her. "That'll take you out of your way. I can manage . . ." I knew she was going to Coeur d'Alene, and Paper Moon wasn't exactly on the way.

Peaches shook her head. "Don't worry about it. It'd only be a little detour. I have a couple of stops to make, but I can get you there early tomorrow morning. I'll drop you off, then hook back up with Montana Route Ten, and catch Ninety going west." She looked at me funny. Blew out a cloud of smoke. "I just have one question."

I inhaled deeply. Loved the smell of the cigarette smoke, even though I was supposed to be quitting.

"What's that?"

"Why Paper Moon, of all places? I thought you left home to find great adventures and excitement and mysterious things . . ." Peaches had the grin of a seven-year-old who's just eaten all of the cookies. "There ain't shit in Paper Moon."

I shrugged my shoulders.

"I ain't never been there. Figured it'd be different from where I came from."

She mimicked me, grinning, and shrugged her shoulders. Blew out more smoke.

"That's as good a reason as any, I guess. You're right, too, it's nothing like Ohio. Just a spot in the road, really. There's a nice lake there, though. Arcadia, I think it's called. There's a Best Western right across the road. Sometimes on the Tulsa to Calgary route I sleep there. The Paper Moon Diner sets close to the interstate, you can't miss it. It's got good food, too. Kinda different but good. The owner's a crazy Indian, though. I heard he got doused with the orange stuff in 'Nam. A few sandwiches short of a picnic, if you know what I mean, but he cooks OK."

I didn't say anything, but it seemed to me that just since I'd been west of the Mississippi, I had heard several comments about Indians, or "Injuns." I was thinking that, out here anyway, Indians had replaced black folk as the "niggers" of the world. ('Course, maybe that's 'cause there aren't any black folk out here.) If that was true, I wondered what it was going to be like to have company at the bottom for a change.

"You sure it wouldn't be out of your way?" I didn't want her to think I wasn't grateful for her offering me a ride, but I hadn't planned on traveling with anyone. Part of the adventure was seeing if I could do it alone. On the other hand, part of the adventure was also meeting people, and having experiences I hadn't had before. And I certainly hadn't ever ridden in a tractor trailer with a woman trucker in the wilds of Montana. Obviously, hitchhiking on Route 90 at night, in the cold, in the middle of nowhere, with nothing but elk and moose and bear for company was an experience I hadn't had either. But I thought I'd let that one pass and take the ride with Peaches instead.

Peaches shook her head.

"Naw, nothing worth mentioning. I'd make up the time anyway when I got back on Ninety. Besides, it'll be good to have the company." She grinned that Kool-Aid grin again. I grinned back.

Paper Moon, here I come.

Chapter Six

I had never seen anything like it. And I haven't since. It was the largest purple object I had ever seen in my life. A huge Kenworth truck cab polished to perfection and gleaming in the warm, early-evening sunlight. Her name was emblazoned at the top just above the windshield: *"Peaches's Purple Passion."*

Lord Almighty. It looked like a giant grape on wheels.

Riding in the cab of an eighteen-wheeler is a lot like being on a runaway train. You can feel the power of those engines beneath your butt, and at eighty-plus miles per hour, you get the very real impression that the whole thing is out of control. You know you've got those eighteen wheels, that huge, roaring engine, and the two-million-ton trailer pushing from behind—and the power is amazing. How Peaches kept control of that monster at such a high rate of speed was beyond me. She left other rigs in the dust. She raced a souped-up IROC-Z—and I didn't even see it in the mirror behind us. The decades-old pickups and jeeps that everyone else drove around here didn't stand a chance. And as for me, I just took deep breaths and held on tight to the strap above my head. And said a prayer. Well, lots of prayers.

Oh Lord, this is Juanita. Please don't let me be smashed into little bits when this thing runs off the road and crashes. Thank you. Amen.

On small hills, I watched Peaches as she ran through the ten gears as if she was painting her nails. Somehow she managed to slow the thing down to forty miles an hour when an asshole in a yellow Tercel pulled right in front of us, then slowed down. I was impressed but she scared the shit outta me. I remember that I put down my thoughts in my notebook with a shaky hand. I decided that I would straighten it out later. It's hard to write neatly when you're traveling eight feet up in a huge truck cab going eighty-five miles an hour.

Peaches glanced over at me, raised her eyebrows, then threw her thirteenth half-smoked Viceroy of the day out the window.

"What are you writing?"

I felt stupid and didn't want to tell her, but then I began to think of my favorite romantic heroines and remembered that they weren't afraid or embarrassed under any circumstances, and this was, after all, just a little adventure.

"I'm . . . well, I'm writing down everything I do and see, that kind of thing," I said. "Keeping a diary, I guess." I closed the little book. I was a little shy about this subject.

Peaches's eyes widened.

"No shit! You're a writer?" she said in amazement.

"I wouldn't say all that," I started. I hadn't ever thought of myself as a writer.

"Are you doing a book? Am I in it?"

"Peaches, it's just a diary kind of thing. Nothing fancy . . ."

"I meet a lot of different kinds of people in my business. But you're the first writer I've ever known. That's really something!" Peaches commented, ignoring me. "If you do a book, you'll leave something behind, a real piece of yourself, a legacy. Like an artist . . . leaving a painting behind for someone to hang in a museum. Not like what I do . . . leaving the aroma of diesel fuel in the air. What kind of a legacy is that?"

"What you do is important. People depend on you to deliver things they need . . ."

"Baby pools for Wal-Mart—I wouldn't call that a necessity, Juanita. No one will die if I don't get the wading pools delivered on schedule. And there's no creativity in it," she said, disgustedly. "Not like what you're doing. That takes smarts. You gotta know what all of those words mean and how to put 'em together. I could barely write a decent sentence in high school," she added, sadly.

I laughed.

"You're giving me entirely too much credit," I told her. "A year ago, it took me three days to read three pages of a book 'cause I didn't know what half the words meant. I barely made it through high school myself. Before I started reading, I used to spend my days watching soaps and talk shows. I'm not literary, or whatever you call it. I'm not intellectual, or whatever that word is. I'm just an ordinary woman. I'm really a nobody."

Peaches inhaled deeply on the cigarette she just lit.

"No, you're Juanita Louis, whole person, who is writing about her life. And it's no less a life than anyone else's. There's laughter, tears, long words and short words, hopes and dreams . . ."

"Just one little dream . . . Besides, I haven't written much. Only twenty pages or so," I said aloud but to myself.

"Well, it doesn't matter, I'm still impressed. What do you have so far? Anything you can read to me? Or is it too personal?"

I told her that it was not, and sifted through the pages of my now coffee-stained notebook until I found the paragraphs about Mrs. Berman and my kids, about the funeral of the little Amish child. I read them to her slowly because the movement of the truck sometimes made it hard to see the words. Then I stopped and waited to see what she would say.

"You're good," Peaches said, softly. "*And* you're wasting your time with this running away stuff. You ought to be sitting at a desk somewhere hitting the typewriter keys."

I chuckled.

"But that's just it! I've never done anything or been anywhere in my whole life. If I don't make this journey, even if it doesn't end in a great adventure, I won't have anything to write *about*." I paused, thinking about the barely breathing existence I had led before. "Besides, I can't type."

"Well, you're still pretty good."

"Thanks," I said. And I really meant it. She had made me feel good. This was the first time I had ever let anyone hear what I had written.

Peaches shrugged, said "That's OK," and puffed on her next cigarette. I looked out the window and stared at a deer that was staring back at me. Saw real mountains in the distance. Began to daydream.

In my mind, I was beginning to see my "past life" in black and white, like TV when I was little. And now, even when I could only see open fields for miles in every direction, I saw brilliant colors for the first time. The wheat was gold, tan, rust, marigold, and taupe. The cornstalks were emerald, lime, evergreen, and teal. The sky was no longer just blue. It was azure or powder blue or sapphire, and the sun's rays were a million shades of yellow or orange. Everything seemed more colorful now. Everything I saw, everything I touched or ate had more depth to it, more life. It had to be because *I* had more of a life now.

No, there was no way I would ever write about the dreary, no-hope existence I had lived before, and I told Peaches that.

She chuckled.

"Well, maybe so," she commented. "But from what I heard, you found a way to bring poetry to some hard times. And the part about the Amish, that was good. See, that's what writers do." She exhaled a thick cloud of smoke. "Don't forget to write about me in your little notebook. See if you can make *my* life into poetry."

I told her that I would try.

Nothing else much happened for a few thousand miles.

And then, I had to pee.

"Not another rest stop for another thirty miles or more," Peaches said when I told her. "Don't suppose you could hold it?" She grinned at me, her cheeks dimpling, her eyes twinkling mischievously, at least they appeared to be as her face disappeared into a cloud of cigarette smoke.

"Not on your life," I said painfully as the truck bounced through a trio of potholes in the highway. I squirmed on the once comfortable seat trying to get situated. I could feel liquid coming out of my pores. I swore to myself that, after this, I would give up drinking Cokes.

"Where is the next spot in the road?" I asked, wondering if there were any towns out here.

Peaches's grin greeted me again.

"Sixty miles or so . . ." her voice trailed off into husky chuckles. She began to move through the gears and I heard the roaring engines whine down. "Keep your drawers on, lady. I'll stop. Take me just a minute though."

I crossed my legs and closed my eyes. I'd keep my drawers on all right. I just didn't want them to be wet.

Peaches pulled off the road alongside a beautiful wooded area just past a stretch of plains grass that seemed to go on forever. I nearly broke my neck and both legs jumping down from the cab, but I couldn't think about that. I caught the roll of toilet paper that Peaches tossed out to me and hobbled quickly into the trees.

As I squatted among the bushes and the wild mushrooms and the berry bush (were those poison?) my momma's voice came back to me. And I remembered a time once, long ago, when I had to go and Momma took me back into the bushes. I couldn't have been more than three or four years old.

"Now squat down low, Juanita, real low, baby." Momma's voice was soft and soothing, the gentle tones of her Georgia country home took all the fear away. "That's a good girl. . . ."

I had been drinking Coke like it was going out of style, so I was taking a good long time. But I was just about finished peeing *and* enjoying my daydream when I heard a sound like somebody blowing out a puff of breath. A really *big* somebody blowing out a really *big* puff of breath.

I froze mid-pee.

Amazing how that happens.

I was afraid to breathe. Afraid to move my head. Afraid. Period. I looked around me as best I could without moving my head. I waited. Then I heard it again, followed by a snort. This time, I could tell where the sound was coming from. And I turned my head.

This time, it was my turn to exhale.

The largest, hairiest, ugliest horse I've ever seen in my life stood only twenty feet or so away. He stamped the ground once with a large foot, then snorted again. Then he looked at me with huge, black, curious eyes.

Then he bellowed. Or howled. Or something. I don't know what the name of that sound was and I didn't stick around to find out. I ran back to the highway and practically flew into the truck cab. I was breathing so hard that I thought I was having a heart attack. I don't even remember pulling up my jeans.

"What the . . ." Peaches exclaimed, startled. "What's the matter with you? You see a ghost or something?"

I tried to explain, but she didn't give me any sympathy.

"A damn elk, Juanita," she said, giggling. "They're all over the place!"

"Biggest horse I ever saw," I gasped, locking the door and looking out the window to see if that giant was following me.

"He wasn't going to charge at you," Peaches said matter-of-factly. "He probably was just warning you away from his territory."

I patted my chest where my heart had pushed through the front of my T-shirt.

"Could have fooled me. He looked real pissed off."

Peaches gave me a sideways glance as she began to work through the many gears.

"By the way . . . where's my toilet paper?"

I started laughing and couldn't stop. Almost peed my pants. Again.

That damn elk could have that toilet paper.

We passed the rest of the trip to Paper Moon in long periods of silence, interrupted by comments from one or the other of us. I was trying to quit smoking, but with Peaches's Viceroy chain-smoking thing going on, I was helpless and the tobacco smelled so good. I gave up—only for the trip to Paper Moon I promised myself—and pulled out a pack of Kools I had stashed in my tote bag in case I got weak. We smoked, drank Coke, and looked at the road and at Montana. And for many miles, that was enough.

Again, I thought about space.

There was a woman on a "Sally Jessy Raphael" show I saw once. She couldn't go out of her house because she was scared of open places, of space. She hadn't even been to the grocery store in fifteen years: Her children went for her, little kids going to the store alone. Maybe I'm getting like her. Like that woman on "Sally."

Afraid of space. Afraid of the world.

Afraid of life.

Well, I'm almost here now. Almost in Paper Moon, Montana.

I guess I'll have to get over it.

Chapter Seven

"Paper Moon, Montana, ma'am, straight ahead."

I woke with a start. Had forgotten where I was, then looked around me. The cab of the truck seemed fuzzy and strange, then I yawned and stretched, blinking my eyes and shaking my head to get the cobwebs out.

"Already?"

Peaches chuckled and elbowed me, hard.

"Already. You've been asleep for over an hour. You've got to remember, there is next to no traffic out here. At night, there's even less. I made good time."

I poured myself some tired coffee and squinted as I looked into the morning sunshine and down the road at a sign: Paper Moon, 10; St. Regis, 55.

"Oh, it's only a paper moon . . ."

Peaches let me off in the parking lot of the Paper Moon Diner with a firm handshake, a bear hug, and a thousand instructions and warnings.

"Remember, Millie Tilson runs a little rooming house/bed

and breakfast of sorts over on Main Street. Shouldn't be too hard to find, Paper Moon only has five streets! And don't forget, this is a truck stop. Some of the guys who pass through here are real assholes—and dangerous. Don't take up with any of 'em. If you want a man, just call me, I know who the decent ones are. The ones that won't beat you, or who aren't married or something." She handed me a grubby business card: "P. Bradshaw Trucking, Inc., P.O. Box 4917, Cheyenne, Wyoming (406) 555-5381."

"Leave a message on the answering machine. Tracie or I will call you right back. You can call collect if you want. I'll tell Tracie, so she'll accept the calls. If you want me to pick you up next time I'm through here, holler. I'd be happy to. I could probably take you to Seattle next month, or down to Dallas if you like that sort of thing. Now, re-member, Fagin's Market's over on Vine in Mason, some-body around here will be happy to give you a lift. The folks in town are a little quiet but nice. Tell Millie I said to treat you right, and not charge you too much. Now are you sure you don't want me to drop you off there? You could leave your suitcases, and then go eat. Or Inez will fix you something. She works for Millie."

My stomach growled.

"Nope. I'm starving. I'll just go on in here and grab a bite first. Then maybe I'll look around a bit." I noticed the mountains though. They were beautiful. And frightening. I really didn't think I'd be looking around much, but it sounded like the right thing to say.

Peaches frowned. She looked worried.

"Are you sure? It's just a hop from here."

"Yes, Mother," I said, taking the tote bag from her. "Stop fussing!"

Peaches blushed and grinned.

"Well, I want you to be OK. So you can finish that book you're working on. I want to read the parts about me." She struck a dramatic pose. "The seductive and mysterious lady trucker, whose smoking eighteen-wheel chariot delivers wading pools to Seattle cherubs." She blinked her eyelashes ridiculously.

I laughed.

"Peaches, you need to quit."

"Call me and let me know how you're doing. OK?"

"OK, quit worrying, will you? And thanks, Peaches. I'd never have gotten here if it wasn't for you."

Peaches blushed again.

"That's what friends are for, Miz Louis. See ya in a few weeks."

She disappeared in a cloud of dust, diesel smoke, and gravel. I had a coughing fit. And after she was gone, I felt a void.

I was alone in the world again.

Like Swee' Pea, about to face the monsters.

I felt as if I'd gone back in time. From the old screen door with the latch hook tapping against the weathered wood, to the 1950s steel-and-vinyl chairs, this place had the feel of another age. Outside, it looked run-down and ancient. A relic from the old West. The "Help Wanted" sign was so old that the edges were curling up. It was off the main highway, on Arcadia Lake Road, sitting at the top of a gentle ravine, which led down to a forest and then to the lake itself.

From the porch, the view was incredible, but a little scary. Huge, towering pine trees of a green color that I'd never seen in Ohio. In the morning sunshine, the lake water sparkled, and I heard birds calling: not little sparrows or robins either. But huge pterodactyl-like things, the kind with wingspans that made strange noises as they flew. There were fishermen on the bank, but I couldn't look down too long. I was beginning to find that heights bothered me, too. All of these phobias. I shook off the dizziness and opened the creaky-looking screen door.

Inside, it was a little better. There were actually plastic red-and-white-checked tablecloths, old-fashioned jukeboxes at some of the booths, animal heads here and there, and photographs of cowboys and Indians. The walls were rough, like the inside of a log cabin (or what I had imagined a log cabin would be like), and the floor, just to be different I guess, was an old burgundy linoleum, ready to be put out of its misery. It was a funny little place but I liked the feel of it. I felt good here. No one seemed to notice much when I walked in. Behind the huge, empty counter area was the cook, baseball cap and white apron on, tending the grill. An old-fashioned cash register sat on the glass counter near the door. Each table had a bud vase containing one tired little carnation straining to suck up a thimbleful of water. On the opposite side of the restaurant sat the only other customers in the place: four elderly men, bent and leathered, drinking their morning coffee and joking with the waitress, who waited to take their orders. They didn't notice me when I came in. It was seven o'clock in the morning. I yawned and opened the menu.

"Coffee?"

"Yes, please." I scooted over into the booth and reached for the cream.

Now, I don't read French. I don't read Italian either. Still don't. (At the time, I thought it was Italian.) Can't even spell Italian, really. I get confused as to where the "i" and the "a" go. In fact, I had *just* learned to read English good not quite a year ago. I looked up and glanced wildly around me. Had this menu been given to me by mistake? Was this a joke? I caught the waitress's eye and she quickly came over, carrying the coffeepot and smiling. She was about my daughter Bertie's age, wearing a "Save the Earth" T-shirt with jeans under her "Paper Moon Diner" apron. Her blue-black hair hung to her waist in one long, thick braid, and she wore silver hoops in her ears. She had a pretty face and friendly light brown eyes.

"Yes, ma'am. Are you ready to order?"

"Uh . . . well, I can't read this menu," I stammered. My face was warm. I felt so dumb. "Did . . . uh . . . is this the breakfast menu?"

"Yes, ma'am," came the polite reply.

"Oh . . . uh . . . do you have any menus printed in English?"

The waitress sighed.

"Afraid not. I can translate for you, though."

OK, I thought. Well, this is the West. Maybe it wasn't in French, maybe it was Spanish. A lot of people probably speak Spanish out here. Of course, I couldn't read Spanish either.

"Oh. OK. Uh . . . what's . . ." I located something that looked as if it might be eggs and bacon. I really had a taste for eggs and bacon this morning. "What's this?" I pointed at some familiar letters.

"Croque monsieur with capers and smoked salmon." Noting my expression (since I didn't have a clue as to what "Croque monsieur" was and the only smoked things I knew about were hams and bacon), she explained that it was, basically, a grilled ham and cheese sandwich.

"Oh. And this?" I pointed out another item. Hopefully, I'd get to bacon and eggs sooner or later. It had to be here somewhere.

"Eggs Benedict."

"What's that?" I asked, frowning.

"Canadian bacon and poached egg on top of an English muffin, covered with hollandaise sauce."

Now, in my mind, there's nothing more pitiful-looking than a poached egg. They don't taste too good either. I looked at the next item. My stomach growled.

"I see." I could tell that she was getting irritated with me, but I was confused. I thought this was a diner. I thought they served plain old food here. In English. What was it Peaches had said about this place?

"Good food. Kinda different, but good."

I stared at the strange words. Obviously, this was what she meant by "kinda different."

"Uh . . . could I . . . uh . . . substitute bacon and eggs, maybe for the muffin and, uh, that Holland sauce?" I asked, hopefully.

The waitress rolled her eyes, and pointed to the bold print at the bottom of the page: "No Substitutions or Additions."

I took a deep breath. I was hungry. I had had only four hours of sleep. My behind was sore from riding in Peaches's cab. I didn't read French or Spanish or whatever it was. And I was starting to get an attitude. Now, I'm generally mild-mannered and easygoing. I don't mess with people, I don't cause trouble or get loud. Unless I'm hungry or tired. Or both.

"Do you *have* eggs and bacon anywhere on this menu?" I asked tightly.

"No, ma'am."

I took a deep breath. Decided to take a different approach.

"Do you have any eggs and bacon in this diner?"

The little waitress looked as if she was about to smile.

I was not amused.

"Yes, ma'am."

"But it's not on the menu." I again stated the obvious.

"No, ma'am."

Well, I was going to get me some eggs and bacon, or be thrown out of Montana.

"Do you have a manager?"

"Yes, ma'am." The smile was barely disguised now.

"Does *he* speak French or Spanish, or whatever the hell this is?"

"Yes, ma'am."

"Can I see him, please, because I don't!"

"*Jess! Jess!* This lady wants to see you!"

She might as well have let out the Rebel Yell. My toes curled and I could feel my hair stand up. My ears were ringing. She gave me a brilliant smile, and turned on her heel, heading across the floor toward the other customers. As I glared after her, I noticed that the cook, who had been tending the grill, turned around, and came out from behind the counter toward me, wiping his hands on his apron.

He wasn't tall and he wasn't short. He wasn't fat and he

wasn't thin. He was about five feet, eleven inches tall, weighed about one hundred eighty or so pounds. He peered at me over his long, hooked nose with curious black eyes. When he removed his Bulls basketball cap, his long black hair, streaked with silver, fell down around his shoulders. He looked at me like a hawk studying a field mouse. I don't know why I remember every detail about his height and weight. Why it was that I noticed the shape of his face, and the strength in his hands as he wiped them on the white apron. He didn't smile. To tell you the truth, he looked kinda mean. But there was something else about him that was getting to me. And I couldn't put a word to it. My stomach flipped a little. Probably because I was hungry.

"I'm Jess Gardiner, the manager. You wanted to see me?"

"Yeah, I do," I told him, trying not to look him in the eye. "Look, Mr. Gardiner. I'm starving. Peaches Bradshaw just let me off here, and she said you'd give me a good meal. But"— I held up the menu—"I can't read this menu. I don't know Spanish . . . I don't know . . . Italian . . ."

"French." He spit out the word.

I stopped and stared at him.

"What?"

"It's French, not Italian," he said abruptly.

My jaws began to get tight.

"Whatever. All I know is, I'm hungry. I want bacon, eggs over easy, hash browns or grits, and some coffee. Now, where is *that* on your menu?"

The black eyes flickered for a second. He looked as if he was about to laugh. What was so damn funny? And I felt myself getting real pissed off.

"We don't serve that. Miss . . ."

"Louis," I snapped. "And it's Mrs." Now, I hadn't even *seen* Rodney Louis in over five years. Don't ask me why today I insisted on being called "Mrs. Louis." Half the time I didn't care.

"Now, I do have an herb omelet, with andouille sausage and a croissant that you might be interested in."

I narrowed my eyes.

"I don't want a damned croissant. I want toast. You know, regular bread, with butter. You put it in the toaster? You *do* have a toaster, don't you? And I don't know what the hell an . . . an-doo-wee, ah . . . sausage is!" Now, normally, I hardly ever loud-talk anybody. But when I'm hungry, or tired—or both—I can make a *Tyrannosaurus rex* look like Little Bo Peep.

"It's a traditional Cajun sausage. You'd like it."

"Since you don't know me, how would *you* know what I would like? Listen, what I'd really *like*, Mr. Gardiner . . ." My voice was beginning to carry. The table of four across the room had stopped drinking their coffee and were practically staring down my throat. The little waitress stood, transfixed, next to the counter, her eyes big, an amazed look on her face. I stopped for a second. Since I was probably the only black woman for eight hundred miles in northwest Montana, I decided to tone it down a bit. Hell, these people might lynch me, dump my body in the forest, and that would be the end of it.

I lowered my voice. Took my time speaking. "What I'd like is eggs, bacon, toast, hash browns, and coffee. If that's a special order, then OK, I'll pay for it." (Like I had lots of money!)

Gardiner's nose twitched and he had a slight smirk on

his face. That smirk was getting on my nerves. I was thinking about doing a neutron dance on his head. "Now, can you take care of that?" I asked.

"We don't serve anything like that. And as you can see, there are no substitutions or additions." He pointed to the bold print at the bottom of the menu. At least *that* was in English. "Now, if you would like for me to make a recommendation . . ."

"If you can make this Eggs Benedine, or whatever the hell it is, surely you can scramble an egg or two?"

Mr. Gardiner's black eyes narrowed again and this time, his jaw got tight. He shook his head firmly, his silver-streaked hair spilling over his shoulders. The smirk was gone, and when he spoke this time, his voice was like ice.

"Look, lady. We don't do special orders, and we don't do à la carte. If it's not on the menu, we don't have it. So if you want bacon and eggs, Mrs. Louis, you'll have to fix them yourself."

Well, what did he say that for? I haven't scrambled eggs, fried bacon, and stirred grits for myself and three growing children for over twenty years for nothin'.

I jumped up from that table faster than you could say "shit" and hightailed it over to the grill. The waitress stared at me with her mouth open, spilling coffee on the counter.

"*Hey!* What are you doing?" the manager yelled after me.

"You said I could fix them myself. That's what I'm do-ing!" I yelled back at him.

"Now, just a minute . . ."

I grabbed a towel, tied it around my waist, picked up the spatula I saw lying near the grill, looked around me, then looked at the waitress. The glint in my eye told her I wasn't in the mood for any crap.

"Eggs?"

"Uh ..." she looked over her shoulder at her manager, who was still standing at my table, his face angry, his
dark eyes fiery. We both looked mean, but I guess I looked
meaner. "In the refrigerator. There." She pointed, and moved
out of my way.

"*Mignon!* Hey, you get outta there! Or I'll come around
there myself and pull you out!"

I looked at him like *he* stole something.

"You lay a hand on me, I'll brain you with this skillet
here!"

I looked at the waitress. "Now get outta my way!" She
jumped aside.

"What the hell? I don't believe this!"

Out of the corner of my eye, I could see Gardiner coming toward me. Although I wasn't the kind of woman to
get into a wrestling match with some man, I would use
that iron skillet if I had to. But just when he'd taken a few
steps, the screen door banged against the doorjamb. I
caught a glimpse of a couple of sleepy children and a man
and woman. In mid-sentence, his tirade changed to "Good
morning, how are you? You can sit here in this booth if
you want. Would you like some coffee? Orange juice for
the kids?"

I pulled out some eggs, found some respectable-looking
Canadian bacon (it would have to do), some *real* bread,
and, way back in the back of the freezer, some hash
browns. This surprised me since Gardiner had acted like
he'd never heard of them. I started frying up the bacon
and hash browns (seasoning them with salt, a sprinkle of
pepper, and some chopped onions), then began to beat
the eggs. I had been whirling around the tiny kitchen like

a dervish for a few minutes, when I realized that I had an audience: the four older men who were at the table across from mine and a teenaged boy who was working at the diner as a busboy. The manager had his back to us, taking the orders of the family that had just come in.

The men stared, greedily, at the bacon and potatoes frying on the grill. I have to admit: that food smelled good. One of the old geezers looked at Mr. Gardiner, glanced at his buddies, then back at Mr. Gardiner, who was now looking my way. Finally, he spoke to me.

"Ah . . . ma'am . . . ah . . . that smells mighty good there. I don't suppose you'd mind scrambling up a few more of those eggs would you? For my buddies and me?" He glanced over his shoulder once more. Caught Gardiner's evil eye. "Now, Jess, I don't mean to be disloyal or nothin', but this stuff smells awful good. And we haven't had a plate of plain old bacon and eggs since you opened this place for breakfast and started serving that French shit!"

His buddies murmured in agreement, but they also glanced fearfully at the manager, who glared silently at them—and at me with piercing, black eyes. Mr. Gardiner did not respond, so the old man shrugged his shoulders and looked eagerly at me. Well, I had stepped in the shit now, so what the hell. I pulled up my hip boots. And since Gardiner wasn't saying anything—silence means consent, right? The worst he could do was have me arrested: for frying bacon and eggs for four old men, one summer school teacher, four tourists from Fresno, and the nineteen-year-old waitress, who was Mr. Gardiner's niece by the way. There were worse crimes.

I started cooking at ten past seven. I barely managed to get my own breakfast fixed and eaten. I didn't get a chance to take a deep breath. Between bites, I cooked for four more tourists who were retired couples from Naples headed to Glacier, five ranchers and two farmers, the owner of the local (and only) gas station, and the busboy, Carl—who was Mr. Gardiner's cousin. I fixed up eggs, bacon, toast, and hash browns, as well as cinnamon toast and pancakes (made from scratch, mind you). I ran out of bacon and one of the customers ran down to the Bi-Lo to get some for me. By the time nine o'clock rolled around, I had cooked breakfast for over thirty people, including four of Mr. Gardiner's relatives! Mignon, the waitress and Gardiner's niece, warned me as she left two plates of pancakes, scrambled eggs, English muffins, sausage (that damn an-doo-wee stuff was all I could find), and bacon at the high school principal's table, that she had overheard her tight-jawed uncle talking "in a real low voice" on the phone to the local sheriff. But I was too busy to care.

"Well, I don't have time to worry 'bout it, honey," I told her as I passed her another plate of hash browns, toast, and bacon for Carl. "I got three orders of pancakes and sausage, and one of cinnamon toast to fill."

It was funny. Gardiner probably woulda thrown me out himself, but the diner got so busy, so fast, that he didn't have time. And everybody that came in started ordering "à la carte" after seeing the plates of bacon, eggs, hash browns, and pancakes I had fixed for Abel Long and the other three old men. Guess they just assumed that's what was on the menu. Since the manager didn't have time to explain that good ole bacon and eggs weren't usually available, he just took the orders and turned them in. To me. I gave him a big smile. He gave me a glare that would stop a train.

At ten, I took a break, poured myself a cup of coffee, and waited for the sheriff to arrive.

I didn't hear him come in. I was slicing tomatoes the size of baseballs and had just yelled at Carl to bring me a stack of clean plates. When I didn't get the plates, heard the screen door slam and the place suddenly get quiet, I turned around.

All of the customers were frozen, mid-bite. And stone-faced Jess Gardiner stood in the middle of the floor next to the biggest white man I had ever seen.

They didn't call him "Mountain" for nothin'.

Frank "Mountain" Peters had to be six feet, twenty-five inches tall and weigh three hundred pounds when he was born. He was dressed in the whole sheriff's getup: khaki pants, black shirt, badge, gun strapped on his hip, crisply starched black shirt, Mountie hat, aviator-style reflective sunglasses. Except for the sunglasses, he looked like a giant-sized Dudley Do-Right.

I didn't know how long he'd been standing there and, frankly, I didn't really care. If he wanted to arrest me, fine. But I had to slice those tomatoes first.

Mignon's eyes were huge as saucers, and I hoped she'd catch herself before she dropped her tray on the school principal. She glanced quickly at her uncle and the formidable sheriff, than looked at me. In fact, everybody in the place was looking at me.

Sheriff Peters made his way toward me, studying the food on the tables as he went. He slowed down when he got to Mr. Ohlson's table. Mr. Ohlson, the principal, smiled sheepishly and balanced a forkful of sausage and potatoes against his beefy fingers, which held a piece of English muffin. He also had something in his mouth.

"Mornin', Sheriff," Mr. Ohlson said as pleasantly as he could. It sounded more like "Mawwumph Shawiff."

Peters tipped his hat slightly, then pulled his sunglasses down to his nose as he took a good long look at Mr. Ohlson's plate.

"Good mornin', Mr. Ohlson. Summer school start up all right?"

Mr. Ohlson swallowed.

"So far, so good," the principal answered, more clearly this time. That man didn't stop eating, though. He just went on sopping up some egg yolk with the muffin.

Jess Gardiner cleared his throat and nodded in my direction. Peters looked over his shoulder, then looked at me. He ambled over to the counter and took off his hat. He left his sunglasses on.

"Ma'am?"

"Sheriff?" My throat was tight. Peters was huge, the size of a walking door. I wasn't sure I wanted to be arrested in little old Paper Moon, Montana.

Then "Mountain" Peters removed his sunglasses and looked at me with an open, eager—and *hungry* expression.

"Frank Peters, ma'am. Jeez, that smells good. And I haven't eaten since six-thirty this morning. I wonder . . . could I trouble you for three eggs over easy, hash browns, toast, six strips of bacon . . . and some of those pancakes?"

Mignon giggled.

"Aw, *Mountain!*" This came from Jess Gardiner, who slapped a towel against his thigh in disgust.

I grinned and reached for the coffeepot and a mug.

"You want coffee, too?" I asked the sheriff, who was now making himself at home, his huge elbows resting on the counter in front of me.

"Yes, ma'am. Thank you. And a large orange juice, please."

"Mountain! You're supposed to arrest her, not place an order!"

"Well, Jess, I can't arrest her on an empty stomach, can I? Besides, I don't see why I should arrest her for anything. In fact, I ought to arrest you if you don't hire her as a cook!" He threw his hat onto an empty stool. "What happened to that 'Help Wanted' sign you had out front anyway?"

"Mountain, that ain't the point . . ." Gardiner started to say.

"Mountain," who'd spied the huge beefsteak tomatoes I was slicing, ignored him. "Oh, and I'll take a couple of those tomatoes, too." He looked sheepishly back at Mr. Gardiner. "If you don't mind."

Laughter followed this comment and Gardiner scowled at Mountain and at me.

"Well, don't ask me anything, I just own the place. Ask Miss High and Mighty over there." He stormed over to an empty table and began to clear the dishes. "She's in charge!" He yelled over his shoulder.

"It's Mrs. Louis to you!" I snapped back, stirring the pancake batter.

"Hummph" was Mr. Gardiner's only response.

With the support of local law enforcement, I decided that I could be bold. Threw a drop of water on the griddle to test it, and yelled at Gardiner, "Will you get me another onion when you bring the plates?" He growled at me and disappeared behind the swinging doors. Mignon giggled again. Within the past hour or so, we had become best friends.

"I should apologize to your uncle," I said, looking toward the still-swinging doors. Now that things had quieted down

a little, and I'd been able to catch my breath, I felt kinda
embarrassed: I had come in here like I owned the place,
disrupted the business, and changed the breakfast menu—
all in three hours! Had practically thrown Gardiner out of
his own diner! Guess he woulda been within his rights to
have me arrested, although from the way Mountain talked,
I felt pretty safe from that. We could hear Gardiner slamming things around in the back. "I don't usually act like
this," I told Mignon. "I guess I was just . . . a little hungry."
I gave the pancake batter another stir. Turned the bacon.

Mignon looked at me sideways.

"I'd hate to see you when you're starving!"

I could feel my cheeks reddening.

"It's a . . . a blood sugar thing," I mumbled.

"Hummph," Mignon commented. She sounded like her
uncle.

"Your uncle's pretty pissed off. I should probably go."

"Why? Jess will get over it. What's he gonna do? Throw
you out?" Mignon motioned toward the twenty or so people who were now eating in the diner. "Sometimes, we
don't get this many customers in a *day* much less for one
meal! I hope you need a job."

I told her that I was really only passing through, but
thanks for the offer. "Besides, Mignon, I can't even read
that French and Italian stuff, much less cook it!"

"It doesn't matter. It's a good thing you came along when
you did. Jess is close to losing this place. Maybe you being here will bring him back to the real world," Mignon
replied, pouring orange juice. "When Mom and Uncle
Jess bought the diner and Jess got this fool idea to turn it
into a Continental haven—in the middle of nowhere—
my mother told him he was crazy."

Mignon's mother, Mary, is Jess Gardiner's older sister,
and his business partner in the diner. I learned that Jess
had picked up his Continental culinary skills in Paris after
he returned from two tours in Vietnam. He had always
wanted to operate a restaurant and when the previous
owner of the Paper Moon Diner decided to retire, Jess
grabbed his chance. The way he figured it, tourists on
their way to Glacier and Flathead National Parks were a
sophisticated group who could appreciate a more Continental type of "cuisine," as Mignon laughingly referred to
it. Jess put the hamburgers, meat loaf, and club sandwiches
out to pasture, and replaced them with eggs Benedict,
cassoulets, and béarnaise sauce. It worked OK for dinner
on weekends. Mignon said that the diner was gaining a
good reputation among the yuppies, university crowd,
and artsy types in Missoula.

But breakfast and lunch were a problem. Mostly locals,
hunters, fishermen, or traveling families with kids then. Only
trouble was, Mignon said, nobody in northwest Montana
was much interested in crêpes suzettes and hollandaise
sauce for breakfast. And hunters and fishermen, and especially families with kids, weren't either. They were, however,
interested in plain old scrambled eggs, bacon, and toast,
pancakes, and other stuff like that, as I had discovered. And
the dinner crowd was iffy—sometimes they were there,
sometimes they weren't. Not a good thing when it came
time to pay the food bills for those expensive Cajun sausages and gourmet coffee beans.

"I told him that his business plan is in trouble," Mignon
added, picking up a plate piled high with pecan pancakes.

I didn't know what a business plan was, so I said "Uh-
huh" in agreement.

"My mother told Uncle Jess that Agent Orange had fried his brains and that he ought to check himself into the psych unit of the VA hospital up near Helena. *I* said, 'Uncle Jess! No one is going to want tournedos of beef at a roadside joint in northwestern Montana! They want plain old steak, mashed potatoes, and green beans! Fried eggs and bacon! Stuff like that!' Mother told him that the only French folks wanted to read on a menu was the à la mode with the apple pie!" She shut up like a clam when her grim-faced uncle returned with a tray of clean dishes—and my Vidalia onion.

"Thank you," I said, taking it from him and trying to keep from smiling.

"Umph," he replied.

I stared after him as he disappeared into the dishroom.

When Gardiner was out of earshot, Mignon grinned and whispered in my ear, "I think he likes you."

I wondered if that was good or bad.

Chapter Eight

News travels faster in Paper Moon than it does in the projects after the talk shows go off.

By eleven-thirty, most of the residents of Paper Moon, and half of those living in nearby Mason, knew that Jess Gardiner had himself a new cook. Thanks to Sheriff "Mountain" Peters and his CB, the lunch crowd was even larger than the breakfast group, and it included some of the same folks! The Paper Moon Diner's regular menu was "temporarily out of service" and an "ad hoc menu," as Mignon called it, was put in place. Foods like "Country Fried Steak," hamburgers, fresh pan-fried trout, and a ten-alarm chili I whipped up in a hurry appeared instead. (One thing Jess *did* have on hand was a large bottle of hot sauce, a decent group of seasonings, some beans, and ground turkey.)

Even with Mignon helping me with the cooking, we had more orders than we could fill quickly. There were so many people coming in that we were all cooking and waiting tables—even Carl, who bussed dishes, scrambled a few eggs and flipped hamburgers. By two o'clock, I was dead on my feet. I hadn't had a shower in two days, and I didn't have a place to sleep yet.

But I did have a job.

Jess asked me himself. At least, that's what *he* thought he was doing.

He passed me on his way to the back, carrying a huge tray of dirty dishes. I was on my way to table eight with four hamburger platters and a fish sandwich. Mignon was taking a ladies' room break.

"Need to be here by six to get ready for the breakfast shift," he said abruptly. "First customers come in at six-forty-five 'fore they go fishing."

I stopped in the middle of the floor.

"You need to tell someone who cares," I snapped. I dropped off my orders and passed him on my way back to the grill.

"Thought you'd like to know," he said pointedly.

I put my hands on my hips and turned around.

"Listen here, the only reason I even *got* behind this counter was 'cause I was hungry and needed something to eat besides crêpes Suzanne or whatever you call them. And the rest of this . . . well, I'm just helping you out is all."

Jess's eyes flickered for a second. And his cheek twitched.

"Guess I was mistaken. Thought you ran the place."

I looked around me. "It would be an improvement. If you want a for-profit business, that is."

"Six o'clock, you can open up."

"Oh, are you offering me a job?"

"Yep."

"I can't make those French dishes you have on the menu,"
I told him. "You're on your own there."

He shrugged his shoulders.

"There's been a reorganization," he said, simply. "New
cook, new menu. You cook what you want. Obviously,"
he looked around him at the full tables and flapping jaws,
"whatever you make will be fine."

And why was I even considering this situation anyway?

I had been complaining for years about spending too
much time on my feet at the hospital. I had been whining
about the hours, bitching about my back hurting (well, that
might have been the extra twenty pounds I was carrying
around but who wanted to go into that?), and moaning
and groaning about the fact that I was tired of low-level
jobs that didn't make any money at all and didn't bring
me any respect or a bank account.

So why was my mouth agreeing to something like this
when my bunions, my back, and my purse were telling
me different?

Cooking.

I love to cook.

I love to eat. (You can see that in my backside.)

So I love to cook.

And not that 6:30 P.M. the kids are starving and crowded
around your ankles yelling "Momma! Is dinner ready yet?"
kind of cooking that you do every day Monday through
Friday either. That shit is for the birds and I did that for
damn near fifteen years nonstop.

Nope. I'm talking about that Julia Child, Gallopin' Gourmet, wearing a big white hat, cooking in a stainless-steel
high-class kitchen kind of cooking. I just love watching

those shows even though I don't have cable and the reception isn't very good.

Not that I need to have fancy pots and pans or recipe books to make *my* food taste good. I can whip up a tuna salad that will make your momma slap you. I can make a pound cake so rich you'll cry when you take a bite and then cry again when it's gone.

I can cook up some collard greens with ham hocks that will make the Pope beg for more. And I can turn a vegetarian into a carnivore with something as simple as my cubed steaks and gravy.

But finally, I just love it when people compliment my cooking. That, for me, is better than sex.

Well, almost better than sex.

And these folks?

They had paid me the best compliments ever.

They had licked their fingers, sopped up egg yolks off the plates, begged for extra potatoes (I was out and had to send one of the truckers out for more), slurped down fresh-squeezed orange drink I made (with oranges, lemons, and tangerines), and wanted to know how long I was staying on so that they could plan their summer.

I loved it.

Just loved it.

And even though my bunion gave me a twinge, I said "quit it" and went on with frying up the bacon.

And I told Jess "Yes," I would stay on until he found someone else.

Mountain told him not to bother to look for someone else.

"What you going to pay me, huh? What are my hours?

What you want me to *do* exactly? I expect to get paid for
the work I've done already," I reminded him. "And remember, I'm just passing through. I'll only be here tempo-
rary. Six, eight weeks at the most." I just stood there looking
at him, cracking my chewing gum. I don't know why I
was so antsy with Jess. He really hadn't done anything to
me. But I didn't want to just stand there, quietly, and just
look him straight in the eye.

Jess stared at me. You could tell that he'd never dealt with
a premenopausal black woman with an attitude before.

Truthfully? I hadn't thought much about a job at all. I
hadn't planned on staying in Paper Moon but a few days.
Just long enough to see what there was to see. And I certainly hadn't planned on being nobody's short-order cook.
But in the last four hours I'd had more fun than I could remember having for a long time—cooking potatoes and
frying hamburgers. The people of Paper Moon came in,
introduced themselves, and placed an order. They seemed
to take it for granted that I belonged here. They thanked
me for the coffee I poured them, complimented me on
the hash browns. Said they had gotten tired of eggs Bene-
dictine. Told me all about their families, their friends, the
affair the chiropractor in Mason was having with the or-
ganist at the Presbyterian church. They acted like I was
just So-and-so's cousin who'd been away for a while and
needed to catch up with the news. And I was enjoying it.
For some strange reason, the whole idea of being a part of
this little spot in the road was beginning to appeal to me.

Jess looked uncomfortable. And even in the few hours
I'd "known" him, I knew why.

I had asked him several questions. He owed me answers. He might even have to use complete sentences. I

wanted to laugh but I couldn't. I could tell that Jess Gardiner didn't like to hold conversations. He wasn't the kind
of man who'd lecture or bend someone's ear. He spit out
instructions, grunted when he was satisfied, growled and
glared when he was not, and used facial expressions and
his eyes to convey the rest. I never knew a man who was
so stingy with words. It was as if he was afraid he would
use them up—and at the rate of four or five a day.

He scowled at me. I scowled back at him.

Then he took my questions—in order.

"Seven-fifty an hour is all I can manage now, but if
things keep going like this, well, I could probably do better in a month or so. Six A.M. to three P.M., or two-thirty,
if things are slow. My sister will do the dinner shift. You'll
be the cook for breakfast and lunch and you can teach
Mignon"—a short pause—"and me some of your recipes.
That way, when you move on, we can manage and maybe
teach someone else. And I'll pay you the seven-fifty for
the hours you worked today."

I kept quiet for a moment. Forgot and looked him
straight in those black eyes. Saw something there I hadn't
seen in a while. Filed it away for later when I had time to
sort it out. After a few seconds, when I figured he'd waited
long enough, I held out my hand.

"It's a deal."

Jess smiled slightly. But his dark eyes were laughing
at me.

"Six o'clock, Mrs. Louis." He shook my hand. With that
done, he quickly walked through the doors to the dishroom. Talking in paragraphs was exhausting for Jess.

"Juanita," I called after him.

"Hummph" I heard him say as the swinging doors closed.

I returned to the counter, my Coke, and my Kools. Mignon sat down on the stool next to me.

"I'm impressed."

"With what?" I said, collapsing onto a stool.

"Uncle Jess doesn't usually carry on a conversation with people unless he's known them for twenty years. I'm only nineteen, so he's only said ten words to me my whole life!"

"That was a conversation?"

Mignon nodded. "For him, it was."

I looked over at the doors, still swinging back and forth. I could see Jess in the back, helping Carl with the dishes.

"I'd hate to hear him when he's not in a talkative mood."

Mignon chuckled. "He doesn't talk to just anyone, you know. Very selective man." She looked over her shoulder, a slight frown on her face. "Momma says he wasn't always that way, though."

"Well, I'll consider myself lucky," I said wearily. "I've gotten your uncle to speak in whole sentences. I have a job. Now all I need is someplace to stay."

"Gee, it's too bad you weren't here last week," Mignon said sadly. "You coulda stayed with us. But now Aunt Pearl and Uncle Ben and their brood are here for a few weeks. We're filled to the rafters."

"What about Millie Tilson's place?" I asked.

Mignon gave me a doubtful look. "What about it?"

"Well, doesn't she have rooms or apartments or something?"

"Yeah, she does," Mignon conceded. "But she's crazy. Thinks she's Jean Harlow or somebody—you never saw anyone like her. Walks around in boas and silk robes in the middle of the day. She's got seven or eight cats and she thinks they're the reincarnated souls of her dead ex-husbands or something. She talks to them all the time like they were people, it's weird."

I didn't remember Peaches mentioning cats.

"Are the rooms clean," I asked, "or does the house smell like cat poop?"

Mignon shook her head, her black braid dancing against her waist.

"No, it's clean. My cousin Ruth stayed there last year while she was going to beauty school. Said it was OK, but Millie talking to those cats got on her nerves."

"All I want is a shower and a clean bed."

"Well, Millie will take you in. She's cheap, too." Mignon looked at her watch. "It's almost two-thirty. If I don't leave now, I'll be late for class. Jess can manage until Momma comes in at four. Come on. I'll run you over to Millie's. It's on the way."

I left my new boss with a grocery list as long as my arm: *real* bacon, ordinary sausage, eggs, frying chickens, pancake mix, stuff like that. I told him to have the food delivered before tomorrow morning or I wasn't cooking. I went over the list, item by item. I think I was getting on Jess's nerves.

"Now, get Oscar Mayer or a good bacon, not none of those off brands that just give you end pieces. And make sure you get plenty of syrup—the real maple kind. Those fishermen like pancakes with their eggs."

"I think I can manage a simple grocery list," Jess barked out, snatching the list from my fingers.

He looked at the piece of paper, grunted, and returned to the grill. Mignon says he's in love.

Millie Tilson's place looks like the Addams Family house from TV. If it ain't haunted, it's on the waiting list. It's got rafters, shutters, a widow's walk, and a porch that wraps around the front and the side. The house is huge, three floors or maybe four. It's Victorian, Georgian, Queen Anne, and Italianate—all mashed up together. It looks as if the architect wasn't sure which style to use, so he used them all. Mignon said it's over a hundred years old. I believe it.

There's a turret at the very top, and as I stood in the street looking up I could have sworn . . . well, more about that later.

I was greeted on the porch by a huge black cat who lay on a wicker rocking chair, blinking his green eyes at me. I spoke to him.

"Hey, Cat," I said.

He blinked back. The front door creaked when it opened. Just like a haunted house.

At first, I didn't see anyone there.

"I see you've met Antonio," came the voice from behind the screened door. "He knew you were coming, of course. He's psychic. You're Jess's new cook, Juanita. I'm so happy to meet you." She held the door open for me. I glanced back at my suitcases. "Just leave them there, I'll have them brought up."

The woman behind the voice didn't introduce herself. She didn't need to.

Millie Tilson was exactly like the house she lived in, except for the boa and the silk robe. She could have been twenty-five or eighty-five. It was really hard to tell. She was a hodgepodge of styles and eras—from the Roaring Twenties to the sixties. She had the blondest hair I'd ever seen, yet it didn't look cheap and brassy. It was cut in one of those thirties styles: short and curled close to the head. Her thin eyebrows were penciled on, her lips painted fuchsia in the shape of a bow. There wasn't a wrinkle anywhere. Her spicy perfume made my nose itch, and reminded me of the incense Rashawn used to burn to cover the smell of the weed. And how she managed to walk in two-inch-heeled mules without breaking her neck I didn't know. And I tried not to stare at the ring on her finger that had an emerald in it the size of a quarter. One thing's for sure, I'd never seen anyone quite like her before in my life.

Millie glided into a little room that reminded me of a parlor I'd read about in a novel about a cattle baron and a madam: Victorian, I think, with heavy, overstuffed red velvet furniture, ornate cherry-wood tables, paisley throws here and there, knickknacks everywhere, plumes of ostrich feathers drooping about, and a huge cat snoozing comfortably on one of the chairs. She shooed the large tabby away with her hand, long nails painted ruby red.

"Louis, go choose the wine for dinner." Obediently, the cat left, and Millie sat down, arranging the folds of her gown around her. "And don't choose a burgundy," she called after him. "We're having poultry!" To me she said, "Please, sit down."

I moved toward a rather large armchair, but Millie stopped me.

"Oh, please, anywhere but there. That's Paul's chair and he's so possessive. He gets furious if anyone sits in his chair, even for a minute!" She motioned toward another large, velvet-covered chair. "There, sit there. That's William's chair. He won't mind. William never minds anything."

I nodded, and sat down, looking around me. Across the

room was a beautiful fireplace, with molded designs in the mantel, and an old-fashioned fire screen in front. The furniture in the room, and there was a lot of it, was like the house—there was a little bit of everything. There were brocaded nineteenth-century fainting couches sitting next to Louis XIV tables; fat cushy Victorian-era settees next to end tables that look as if they had been designed by Salvador Dali. The drapes were paisley and red velvet— ugly but interesting. And tucked away in one of the few empty spaces was a two-drawer beige steel filing cabinet, hopelessly out of place but obviously useful.

Dominating the room was a large painting. No matter where else you looked or what you looked at, your eyes always came back to that painting. It was above the mantel and it was a large portrait of Millie Tilson, painted when she was much younger, judging by the long, curly dark brown hair that hung past her shoulders, and by the fact that she was completely naked, lying on a velvet-covered settee, which looked a lot like the one she was sitting on now. I quickly looked back at the real Millie.

"Oh, do you like that portrait?" Millie asked me. "Taubert painted it for me in Paris while I was married to the count. Of course, we had an affair during the sittings." She sighed and smiled wistfully. "That's why I look so relaxed, you know." She changed gears in a split second. "Now what can I do for you?"

"I . . . uh . . . Mignon Nightwing and Peaches Bradshaw told me that you might have rooms to rent . . ." I stopped when I noticed that Millie Tilson had pulled a tiny laptop computer out from under a pillow and was busily tapping the keys. Her black reading glasses trimmed in gold were perched on her nose. "I wondered if . . . uh . . . if I could talk to you about renting one . . ."

"You may have the . . . Mauve Room, second floor, third door on your left," she interrupted me. She tapped a key, then sat back and studied the screen. "It's vacant now, thank goodness. Had a nice couple in there for the weekend, she's a systems analyst from Boise, he's a broker from Missoula. Both married, but not to each other, obviously. *I* could tell. They were rather noisy. . . ." The computer beeped. She looked at it and frowned. "How long will you need the room?" She didn't wait for me to answer. "You'll have to share a bath with Jewell Matthews, but that shouldn't be a problem. Jewell's on a walking tour of England until the end of August. And she's a schoolteacher, quiet woman. Sexually repressed, of course." The computer beeped again. Millie tapped another key, and nodded in satisfaction.

"Perfect, I've got you all set up. Since you're working for Jess, we'll just leave your departure date open, shall we?"

I didn't know what to say. I'd never faced an octogenarian femme fatale psychic who was a computer hacker before.

"Of course, you might also like the Tower Room . . ." Millie murmured to herself rather than to me. "It's got the Widow's Walk, you know. Lovely view. I'd have to obtain Elma Van Roan's permission first. But she probably won't mind. Just doesn't like men much. Gave the doctor from Denver no end of trouble."

"Elma Van . . ."

She slipped the pair of half glasses back on as she pulled up an accounting ledger or something on the screen. Her fingers flew across the keyboard. Her nails clicked noisily.

"Van Roan. Elma's the ghost who lives on the third

floor. She's partial to the Tower Room—she and Reverend Van Roan slept there back in the eighteen eighties."

"The Mauve Room will be fine," I said quickly, not wanting to disturb Elma. In fact, now that I knew there was a ghost in the house, I wasn't sure I wanted to stay here at all.

She quoted me a rate that even I could manage on what Jess was paying me. "That will include the room, housekeeping, and meals on your off days, the run of the place. You're responsible for your personal laundry, Inez will take care of sheets, towels, and so forth, but you have to carry them to the basement. Local calls are free but I'll bill you for long distance."

I asked her what I owed her for the deposit and counted it out into her hand. As she wrote out the receipt, a huge, white long-haired cat sauntered into the room. Millie stopped writing and smiled. The cat strolled over to her, rubbed against her leg, and purred loudly. Millie gave a husky laugh and stroked the cat under his chin.

"You devil. It's not nice to remind me about that," she said coyly, as if talking to a . . . well, a real person. Her cheeks colored brightly. "Juanita, this is my fourth husband, Paul Hillman Daniels. He was just telling me how fondly he remembers our trysts on this settee I'm sitting on, the rogue. Paul, you are too much!"

I said nothing, and nodded. Living at Millie Tilson's would be different.

Millie Tilson's mansion operated as a bed and breakfast/rooming house and it seemed to be making her some money. Tourists used it as home base for trips into the national forests around here. Honeymooners liked the Tower Room for those special nights. And ordinary folks, like me, used it as a "boardinghouse" kinda place. There's room for everyone. And as cozy as it is, it's pretty huge, so you can be alone when you want to or be up under people when you want to.

I guess "mauve" means pinkish, 'cause Millie's Mauve Room had wallpaper on the walls with a border that was pinkish in color with tiny flowers. The pink draperies hung from ceiling to floor and were swept up on the sides. There was a huge poster bed in the center, with a white chenille-like bedspread, and a pillow on it that had letters. Needle-point, I think it was. I leaned closer to read it: "Wild Women don't get the blues." I wondered who had stitched it. Millie Tilson *had* been a "wild woman" in her younger days, but I couldn't picture her sitting still long enough to do needlepoint. The dresser was covered with lace doilies and a vase of flowers was set at the end. I gently touched one of the petals. Real flowers.

I had never had a room like this. I had never even seen a room like this. I read about four-poster beds and fresh flowers in vases, but it hadn't been a part of my life—until now. I fell back on the bed and looked at the ceiling. It was domed, and sculptured with flowers, too. I had found a romantic heroine's paradise way out here in little Paper Moon, Montana.

I closed my eyes.

I wondered what kind of heroine I would be. I tried to imagine myself in the Regency, but that didn't work for me. The Colonial era wasn't appealing—everyone knows that the Puritans had no sense of humor and were no fun at all. The 1860s had their own issues. The Roaring Twenties might be fun. Or maybe the 1880s in the West, like where I was now. I thought about how I would look with bobbed hair, or wearing chaps herding cattle on horse-back. Both prospects were pretty funny. I decided just to be myself in the present and see where that road took me.

I ended my little daydream, pulled out my notebook, and tried to take in all that had happened to me since the day before yesterday.

Chapter Nine

Paper Moon was about the tiniest place I'd ever seen in my life. Considering that I hadn't ever been anywhere.

The town is perched on the hillside of a small mountain, which sits at the bottom of a big mountain, surrounded by a dense forest, so all that's visible from a distance are the steeples of its two churches.

The center of town has only two main streets, some stores, the churches, and a gas station. Everything looks like it's left over from the last century: small, white, green-shuttered houses, and gas pumps like I've only seen in old movies. Many of the people around here farm, work at the Wal-Mart in Mason, or commute to Missoula, which is east and over an hour away. Not much industry in Paper Moon, although a paper plant just north of here stinks up the air a lot. Some folks work up there and the plant runs two shifts.

And that's another thing I've noticed about this part of the country. The distances! People will drive long distances at the drop of a hat, and for no reason at all. It's nothing for Mignon to drive four hours just to go shopping. I guess they're used to it. Montana is such a long, empty state, it takes at least two hours to get anywhere. I had a lot to get used to.

The Paper Moon Diner sits off the highway on the edge of town, across from a tired-looking Best Western and the gas station. It's noisy in the front because the trucks roar past on their way north toward Captain or Glacier, or east to hook up with I-90 and Missoula.

But I would come in the back way, and from the porch you could see Arcadia Lake at the bottom of the hill, quiet and blue. The birds called to each other, and there was almost always a deer or two looking around, then bending their graceful necks to get a drink. The lake is surrounded by huge pine trees and the quiet beauty of it mystifies me every morning when I open up. I take my breaks out here. Probably will until it gets too cold, if I haven't moved on by then. But then, after seeing all of this, I don't know if I can go back to a city of concrete and steel.

When I opened the diner that next morning at six, my second day in Paper Moon, I found a note from Jess on the counter. He told me that he had bought the food I asked him to and put it away in the pantry (in the back) and in the refrigerator, which was behind the counter. He told me that his young cousin Carl would bus and wash dishes until noon. He told me that Mignon worked Monday, Wednesday, and Friday, 6:45 to 2:45; that Rosetta Hanson worked Tuesday, Thursday, and Saturday, same hours. He said he'd be in by 6:30. Had the nerve to ask me to fix him an omelet with onions, tomatoes, and mushrooms in it. Told me where to find the change for the cash register and that Roy Porter, Abel Long, Fish Reynolds, and Bud Smith would arrive for coffee at seven sharp. In fact, Jess's little note was downright chatty—for him. He told me just about everything I needed to know.

But he forgot one thing.

He forgot to tell me about Dracula.

I opened the diner with the keys Jess left in the fourth geranium pot on the right in front of the handicapped parking space on the side of the diner. I came in, locked the door behind me, and turned on the lights. Fiddled with the dial on the old radio at the end of the counter until I found the only station in the area that didn't play country and western, then read Jess's note. I pulled out the bacon and sausages, left them on the counter to soften, washed up and got an onion to chop for the hash browns I knew Abel Long liked. Had just put two pots of coffee on and was about to light me a Kool when I heard it.

Soft, sliding, clicking sounds in a rhythm coming across the floor toward me. I froze and a lump formed in my throat.

I was not alone.

There was someone—or something—else here.

"It."

Lord, I didn't want to think what kind of wild beasts might live in Montana. Wolves? A bear? I shivered. Felt my blood run cold.

I couldn't imagine how it had gotten in—whatever it was—since the doors were locked this morning and I hadn't seen any windows broken. But there was no time to think about that now.

I didn't want to turn around without a weapon, so I

grabbed the big iron skillet from the back of the stove, and held it tight. In the corner of my eye, I could see the front door of the diner. I tried to figure out how far away "It" was in case I had to make a run for it. Then I turned around. Slowly. Gripping that pan like it was a baseball bat, I held my breath.

There, in the middle of the floor, stood the biggest, blackest, most vicious-looking rottweiler I'd ever seen in my life. His tongue was out and his eyes were glued—on me. I tightened my grip on the frying pan. I was scared shitless. I knew that those dogs could rip your throat out and tear you into bits. I said a quick prayer and braced myself for a fight. The dog studied me for a moment, then lunged.

It was over in two seconds.

I was tackled and knocked to the floor by a one-hundred-pound hush puppy who tried to lick my face off (yuck!) and wanted me to rub his stomach and scratch him behind the ears. He was so cute. I found myself giggling. Now, I haven't giggled for twenty years.

The screen door slammed and I heard Jess's voice.

"I see you've met Dracula."

"I ought to knock you out," I growled at him (not seriously) as I picked myself up and dried my jeans off with a kitchen towel.

His eyes widened and he looked surprised.

"What did I do?"

"Nice of you to tell me you had a guard dog. He coulda killed me!"

Jess grunted.

"Yeah, well, you don't look too bad off. Like you've been licked to death, that's all."

"That's beside the point," I shot back, still grinning and scratching that fool dog behind the ears. "He's a rottweiler. He's an attack dog. Aren't you, Dracula?" I crooned. Jess rolled his eyes. Dracula closed his in ecstasy. "He's supposed to tear throats out and rip men to shreds. Aren't you, sweetie?" The hardened attack dog nuzzled my hand enthusiastically.

I could tell Jess was not convinced.

"Hummph. That dog never hurt anybody in his whole life, and everybody around here knows it. I only keep him in the diner at night on the outside chance that some foreigner tries to break in. I figured maybe Dracula would scare him off."

I looked at Dracula's eager brown eyes as I petted him on his large, boxlike head.

"I don't think so," I told Jess. "I coulda walked off with everything. He didn't even bark."

Jess whistled and the dog came running, tongue out, tail wagging eagerly.

"Likes women for some reason," he grumbled, kneeling down and patting Dracula vigorously. The dog was in hog heaven. "Don't know why."

"We smell better," I said, washing my hands, sniffing the air. Something hit my nose like a boulder. There was a definite stench there. It was coming from Jess's direction and, whatever it was, it wasn't gonna go well with my scrambled eggs and waffles. "Speaking of smell . . ." I walked slowly toward him and the odor got stronger.

Jess looked around innocently wrinkling his nose.

"I don't smell anything."

His dark eyes twinkled. His expression was serious but his eyes were laughing at me.

I held my nose.

"Whew, it's no wonder! What have you been doing? You smell like shit!"

Jess chuckled. Something I thought I'd never hear.

"Manure, Mrs. Louis. Manure. Delivered some to my sister this morning. She's putting out flowers, needs to add it to her beds."

I scratched my nose.

"Manure, shit, whatever. Either way, you need to get out of here before you stink up the place and run all my customers off." I fanned a towel at him. "Shoo! Go on, get out of here!"

He beamed at me with a wide, lopsided grin that reminded me of a scarecrow standing in a cornfield I'd passed back in Indiana. It was a silly grin, but nice. I smiled in spite of myself. I had gotten the feeling that Jess Gardiner was as stingy with his laughter and his smiles as he could be with conversation. Thought I'd better take advantage of it while it lasted. Encourage it if I could.

"Your customers? I thought I was the boss of this place," he said with a raised eyebrow.

"There's been a reorganization." I held my nose and fanned the towel again. "Now get out and take a shower. And don't take forever. Omelets don't keep that good."

"Umph," said Jess, still grinning. He and Dracula disappeared out the back door. I chopped up my onions, mixed up some pancake batter, and heated up the griddle. Scrambled eggs for myself and Carl, made Jess's omelet, and toast. Fried up two pounds of bacon. I was finishing my first cup of coffee when Abel Long walked through the front door with his wife, his mother-in-law, and his chiropractor at seven A.M. sharp. He wrinkled his nose, and sniffed the air a little. I tried not to laugh. Then Abel said "Hey, Juanita!" and ordered the works for everybody. And it went on from there, just like I had lived in Paper Moon, Montana, all my life.

I opened the diner at six forty-five every morning, went off duty at two-thirty, took off on Sundays for sure (since the diner was closed) and one other day of my choosing. Since I wasn't used to having a choice about much of anything, I worked six days straight the first two weeks I was there. Mignon had to remind me that slavery was illegal in the United States and assigned Mondays as my "off" day.

I practically ran the diner. Folks around here, and the truckers and the tourists and the state police, loved my cooking, so Jess had no problem with anything I did. Mignon said he made more money in the first two weeks I was here than he had for the past two months. Jess didn't say thanks directly.

But I did get my raise.

I changed the menu to "home style/Southern" for breakfast and "reg'lar food" for lunch. Mignon and one of her friends designed new menus on the computers at the community college. They call it "Juanita's Meal Deals." Eggs, bacon, sausage, hash browns, grits (I send away to Georgia for these), etc. are standard fare. Lunch is mostly hamburgers, chili, and fish sandwiches if I can get the fillets fresh. Dinner is Jess's shift, and I leave that pretty much alone. He manages to get a respectable crowd for dinner even if he does serve food I can't pronounce. A lot of the artsy crowd drive up from Missoula, and we do get tourists who consider themselves "sophisticated" and familiar with "nouvelle Montana Continental cuisine," as Jess calls it. (Whatever the dickens *that* is.)

Rosetta got strep throat the third week I was here, so I worked the dinner shift for a couple of nights. Just about drove Jess crazy and almost got myself fired. But I had fun. Couldn't keep a straight face all night. I'd forgotten how much fun giggling could be.

I can't pronounce half of the stuff Jess has on his dinner menu. I watch him cook it up and most of it looks pretty and smells really good. It tastes good, too, though I hate to admit it. But the names of these dishes are just beyond me, with their "oh juice" this and "flambay" that and every other word being a "de." I get all tongue-tied. And those were the easy ones. That was bad, since it was part of my job to tell the customers about the nightly specials. Actually, I did all right until Thursday night. Then Jess decided to get fancy. And I got stuck on some of the words.

Like "shiitake" mushrooms, for instance.

I knew I was in trouble when the diners came in. "Yups" I call them. You could tell by the skinny, wire glasses the man wore, the plaid walking shorts the woman wore, and the perfect, precise way that they looked at the menu, as if they were going to take notes in class. The man made a big show about ordering the wine, sniffed the cork every which way, and swished the wine around in his mouth like he was using Listerine. I thought he was going to pull out a toothbrush. His wife beamed at him like a head-lamp. Behind their backs, Mignon pretended to stick her finger down her throat.

Then, it came time to go over the menu. I brought

their drinks and took a deep breath. I had been having trouble with this one item all night.

"I'd like to take a minute to go over this evening's specials if I may. Chef has prepared rainbow trout with a lemon bernaise sauce with shallots, herb rice, and asparagus. The trout is fresher than fresh—caught today." And that was no lie—Abel Long had reeled them in around eight this morning. "And the tornados of beef sirloin served . . . oh . . . oh . . ."

Damn. This was the part I hated most. Couldn't remember if they were "tornados" of beef or "tornedos" of beef. Either way, I was confused. They just looked like steak pieces to me. And the "oh juice" part was a problem, too. I had been fumbling with the words all evening. I decided to give it up.

I cleared my throat and started again.

"Sorry. Tornedos of beef sirloin, served with juice, spiked with a little wine, and not that cheap bootleg homegrown stuff either, Chef is using a special California Merlot; steamed green beans with sweet butter and lemon, and wild rice with shitty mushrooms." There. Finished. Glad it was over, I exhaled.

"Excuse me?" Mrs. Yup's eyes were as big as saucers. Mr. Yup's wine had apparently gone down the wrong way, and he was coughing.

"I'm sorry, could you repeat that last item? I didn't quite catch what you said. Wild rice with . . . what?"

I took a deep breath and started again.

"Wild rice with shitty mushrooms, the oh juice has wine in it," I repeated. "Salads are à la carte, and we have two of them. A Caesar and a fresh spinach salad with warm honey bacon dressing."

I smiled. Mr. Yup was still coughing and turning red. He reached for his water glass. Mrs. Yup looked like she wasn't feeling well.

I smiled.

"Would you like to order now?" I asked politely.

They ordered the trout and two spinach salads.

By eight o'clock, the place was packed, and Jess was in a tizzy. Just about everybody had ordered the trout or the lamb roast, which was disappearing in a big way. He had tornedos of beef coming out of his ears, but nobody was ordering it.

Jess caught me returning from the Yups' table after dropping off their dessert. One of those "flambay" things: pretty to look at but not much there.

"Juanita, I'm in a situation here," he told me, a worried look on his face. "No one is ordering the beef. I don't understand it. It's one of my best dishes."

I shrugged my shoulders.

"Can you try to talk some of them into getting the beef? I'm gonna run out of trout if twenty more people order it!"

"Well, if you ask me, it's those shitty mushrooms you're serving with it," I told him, tossing the Caesar salad for the two couples who were sitting next to the old stove. "I don't care what you say about these Continental dishes, Jess. Nobody wants to eat something that sounds funny. What kind of mushrooms got shitty in its name? What's the matter? What's so funny?"

Jess's sister, Mary, who was also working that night, was grinning from ear to ear, tears coming out of her eyes. Jess was doubled over the counter, his head in his arms. I could tell by the bobbing of his body that he was laughing.

"What's so funny?" I asked. "What is it?"

"What . . . what did you call those mushrooms?" Jess asked, coughing as he laughed.

I narrowed my eyes.

"Shit-tay. I pronounced them just like you told me to. With the 'e' on the end, which sounds like 'a' in French, you pronounce them 'shit-tay.' " I looked at Mary, who now had tears streaming down her face, and at Jess, who could barely stand up. "It *is* French, isn't it?" I asked, now suspicious. It *looked* French.

"Juan . . . Juanita, it's Japanese or maybe it's Korean. I've forgotten which. They're known as 'Chinese black mushrooms.' Anyway, it's 'shee-tah-kay' mushrooms, not 'shit-tay' mushrooms. No wonder people haven't ordered the beef. You've been telling them that the mushrooms are shitty!" He was laughing so hard his face was turning red.

Of course, I didn't think any of this was funny. But we did sell a lot more of the beef tornedos after that.

I called home one evening shortly after that, after my first month or so in Montana. Rosetta had gone home early because her little boy was sick, and I filled in for her. Fortunately for me, the crowd was light, and Jess's menu was pronounceable.

"Give me change for a five, Jess, I'm gonna make a phone call."

"You can use the phone in the office."

"No, I don't want it on your bill. The pay phone will do just fine."

"If there's a more stubborn woman around, I don't know her."

"Just give me the quarters, Jess."

He shrugged, punched a few keys. The register dinged, and the drawer opened. Jess handed me a fistful of quarters.

"Long distance, huh."

"As if it's any of your business, yes. Calling my kids back in Ohio."

Mignon flew by with a tray overloaded with dirty dishes. The diner was closed, and she was rushing because she had a date.

"I didn't know you had any kids, Juanita. How many do you have?"

"Three, ages twenty-five, twenty-three, and twenty," I answered, shortly, heading toward the pay phone. "Two boys and a girl, in answer to your next question."

"Hummph," said Jess. In Jess's language, that means "very interesting."

"I bet you're a great mom," Mignon remarked, washing her hands. "They probably miss you, huh."

I thought about Bertie sitting on the couch, asking me for cigarette money, telling me to watch Teishia so she could go out. I thought about Randy sitting in the penitentiary, watching the calendar. I thought of Rashawn, and the apple-sized bankroll he kept in his pocket. No, I wasn't a great mom. And I doubted if they missed me at all. My throat got a little tight, and I quickly turned away toward the wall and picked up the receiver of the phone. But not before I caught Jess's eye.

"Not really." I dialed the familiar number.

I got Rashawn, who was still pissed off. He cursed at me. Said that Randy called . . . something about him getting out. I knew I was hearing things. Rashawn said I was selfish and stupid for "runnin' off like that." He said Bertie and the baby were fine and was I going to send them some money. I said he could give them money; shoot, he makes more in one night than I ever did in a week. He told me to forget it, that was "business." I hear the way he talks to me, see his flashing gold eyes in my mind. I wondered what I did wrong with that boy and why was he so mean. Rashawn asked for the number here, but I wouldn't give it to him. Told him I didn't know it. Rashawn said, "Momma, are you so stupid, you can't axe someone?" I told him I'd call again in a few weeks and hung up. Ignored Jess who was watching me out of the corner of his eye.

I put down the pay phone and came back to the counter. Waved at Mignon, who had grabbed her stuff and was headed out the door. Sat down on a stool and lit me a cigarette. I must have looked a little blue. I felt Jess watching me as he swept the floor but I ignored him. Heard him fumbling around with something in the utility closet.

I thought about Randy in jail. Wondered if Rashawn would live to be twenty-five and if he'd ever give up dealin'. Wondered if I'd been a good mother to Bertie. Couldn't think of any good answers. Couldn't think of any answers at all.

"You OK?" Heard the swishing of the broom, back and forth.

I blew out the smoke and nodded. Thinking hard.

"Yeah."

"Kids all right?"

"Yeah," I answered him in a low voice. My face still

stung from Rashawn's heavy voice and mean words. I felt as if he had slapped me. I didn't look up at Jess. Just blew the smoke out. Studied the glowing orange tip of my cigarette and felt like I wanted to crawl under the counter and stay there for a week.

"You've got three of 'em, right?"

I looked up.

"Yeah."

"Two girls and a boy? Or two boys and a girl?" His question was left hanging in the air as I felt anger—and shame—rise up in my chest.

What the hell was this? Twenty questions?

Just all of a sudden, I was mad as hell.

"You doin' a background check on me, Jess? A little late, ain't it? What is it you really want to know? Let's just stop fartin' around here and get to it!"

I was shouting now and Carl, who was in the back finishing the dishes, peeked over the top of the swinging doors, his eyes wide, his eyebrows raised.

Jess stopped wiping down the counter.

"Juanita . . ."

I stubbed my cigarette out so hard into that ashtray that I broke my nail down to the quick.

"Three kids, two boys, one girl. Randy's in the state penitentiary and I don't know when he'll get out. Rashawn is an entrepreneur—he sells recreational drugs to the rich kids in the suburbs and to the poor kids down the street. Bertie is a stay-at-home mother, and I have one grandchild, Teishia. And I left because I couldn't stand it anymore. I felt like I was all worn out, emptied out, torn up, fed up, and used up. That tell you what you want to know?" I caught sight of something out of the corner of my eye. Carl. Still peeking at us over the top of the doors.

"Carl, do I need to come back there?"

His head disappeared.

"No, ma'am," I heard him say.

Then I turned my wrath back on Jess. But his expression was still calm and he looked as if he was slightly amused.

That ticked me off more.

"Juanita, I wasn't trying to get into your business. Just making conversation . . ."

I lit another cigarette and glared at him.

"Well, this is a conversation I don't want to have."

"I can understand why you left."

"I don't think so," I bellowed, blowing the smoke out in his direction. "And we are not having this conversation."

Jess chuckled.

Chuckled!

I felt the color rising in my face.

He was laughing at me?

"Is there a joke or something that I didn't get the punch line to?"

"Juanita, I . . ."

I hopped off that stool in a flash and confronted him, my hands digging into my hips. That fool cigarette fell out of my mouth and onto the floor.

"Don't 'Juanita this 'n' that!' " I was shouting now. "I guess you think it's pretty damn funny. And pretty damn typical, huh? One son in the pokey, one on the way?"

Jess's eyes widened for a moment, but he didn't answer right away. 'Course, he couldn't. I was still screaming at him.

He came around the counter and grabbed me. I was so

startled—he moved so quickly! I swatted at him and pushed him away.

"Juanita, I wasn't laughing at you. But you're right, I was thinking about how typical your situation is. Too damn typical."

I glared at him.

But I was listening.

"You think your neighborhood has the market on young men wasting away in state prisons or dealing drugs? You think you're the only sad, beaten-up woman who's wondering what she did wrong? The rez is full of mothers like you."

I was still listening.

And I knew that I wasn't the only one. I guess that I never thought there were so many of us. And I was very busy feeling sorry for myself.

But my old belligerence came back. I cocked my chin up at him. I know I had a glint in my eye.

"If this is such a sad story that you've heard so many times before," I challenged him, "then why were you smiling like it was something funny? Or cute?"

Jess chuckled.

I liked the sound of Jess's chuckles. And I wasn't minding too much the feel of his warm hands against my skin.

"You don't read me too well," he said, beginning to grin. "I wasn't laughing at you, or at your situation. I was laughing because you had the nerve to try to do something about it."

I just stared at him.

Then I pulled away from him. Reached for the pack of cigarettes that I'd left on the counter. I was smoking too much. Again.

My heat was gone.

My anger was suddenly gone, too.

Now I just felt sad again.

I sank down onto one of the stools next to the counter.

The sound of the match striking was as loud as thunder in my ears. I closed my eyes and inhaled deeply.

"Most people wouldn't call leaving home a solution, Jess," I said in a smoke-filled voice. "They would call it walking out on your responsibilities."

"How old are those kids, Juanita? Twenty-two? Twenty-three? Isn't it time for them to try life without you?" He snorted caustically and went to get the mop. "I call it saving your own life. Those kids are young, they'll figure it out." The utility closet door slammed. Something in there rattled again. "Or they won't. But you and me, we're working on the end of the story now." The mop made a soft, wispy sound on the old linoleum floor. "We don't have a lot of time to fool around trying to figure out which party to go to." He stopped mopping for a second and looked over at me, his black eyes serious and penetrating.

"We got to pick a party and go."

I looked away.

What party had I picked exactly?

I felt his eyes studying me but I wouldn't look up. I heard the soft, swishing sound again.

I didn't say anything. Listened to the sounds of the old Hobart dishwashing machine running in the back, and Carl's rap music playing on his cassette player.

"Well, you feeling OK? You don't look so good. Take your pill today?"

I shook my head. Maybe I should go back, I thought.

Maybe I ought to be watching Teishia so Bertie could have a little fun in her miserable life.

Or maybe I should listen to Jess.

"Naw. I'm fine."

"Husband misses you, huh." Swish, swish, swish.

I blew out the smoke again. Shook my head, no. Maybe Rashawn was right. What was I doing here? What right did I have to try to have a life without trying to help my kids? But then I *had* tried to help my kids, hadn't I? Hadn't I? They were grown now, and had to make their own ways. God knows, they had never listened to anything I tried to say. I went back and forth with myself.

I was so wrapped up in my thoughts, that I barely heard Jess's voice. Heard the words, and answered him, but didn't really catch the meaning. Then it came through to me what he was really asking.

"Sorry?"

Swish, swish, swish.

"I said, your husband misses you, probably wants you to come back."

I turned around to look at Jess. Found two very black, very curious eyes studying me carefully. I decided to study him back.

"Jess, I ain't had a husband in seven years. Now you knew that."

"Hummph." Jess's cheeks colored. I like that in a man. He quickly looked down at his mopping. I took a long draw on my Kool. Began to think of things I hadn't thought of in years. I decided to play along.

"I know Miz Gardiner wishes you'd quit this diner foolishness and get a real job." Now I *knew* there wasn't no Mrs. Gardiner, Mignon had made sure that I knew that.

Black eyes flickered for a second.

"Ain't no Mrs. Gardiner."

I turned around on that stool. Smiled to myself and watched the smoke curl up in a silver ribbon to the ceiling.

"Hummph," I said. Very interesting.

Jess? And me?

I heard that mop go "swish, swish." Dreamed a little dream.

I called Peaches that night, too, left my name and where I was staying on her answering machine: "Hello. P. Bradshaw Trucking Company. Your message is important to us. Please leave your name, telephone number, date and time of your call, and we will return the call promptly. Thank you."

I closed up that night. Jess just left me there, sitting on that stool, smoking and thinking. About what had changed. And what hadn't. And about the party that I had decided to go to.

Life at Millie's was not like life anywhere. I was one of three permanent "boarders" as she called us—me, the teacher who was out of town for the summer, and an Episcopal priest who was working out of a storefront church in Mason. I could do what I wanted as long as I didn't "do it in the street and frighten the horses" as Millie says. *And* as long as I didn't bother the cats—or the ghost.

Mignon was right about Millie's cats. Millie talked to them constantly. And the funny part was, they seemed to understand her—and talk back.

It's crazy to think of these animals as reincarnated exhusbands, but when you live at Millie's, it's easy to fall into that trap. Stay with her a couple of days and you'll start talking to the cats, too.

The small, mild-mannered gray one was William, Millie's first husband, who was a seventy-year-old English lawyer when she married him in London. She was twenty-six. I guess his family threw a fit. William was an easygoing, lazy little cat who liked to sleep on the window seat in the parlor. He only really springs to action when Millie calls him to eat. She says that her husband used to sleep during his legal trials, but that he was a nice old man. Left her a fortune.

Antonio is a sleek, black short-hair, long on temperament, short on litter box skills. He doesn't like me for some reason, so we stay out of each other's way. Millie calls him "Romeo Antonio" and chides him for his wanderings, which have left him with descendants as far away as the next county. The real Antonio was also quite a character, according to Millie, who divorced him after she found him carrying on in her bed with her best girlfriend and the butler.

Louis is a tabby: friendly, fat, and lively. According to Millie, his human counterpart was a count whose vineyards in Provence were declining in fortunes until she arrived and helped him develop a new wine with a different mixture of grapes, or something like that. The wine was a success, and Millie and Louis got rich. He and Millie divorced on good terms after he found *her* in his bed with the butler. Of course, she was also seeing the portrait painter at the time. Now that's a story I'd like to hear more about. Louis is my boy. He and I share the porch swing in the afternoons, and he eats kitty snacks from the palm of my hand.

Paul is the white Persian, fat, spoiled, conceited, and disagreeable to everyone but Millie. Paul doesn't know that he's a cat now and not an oil baron. At dinner, he sits at the head of the dining room table and Millie serves him his dinner there. Believe it. Paul Hillman Daniels was a Texas oil baron and Millie's last husband. I think it's his money that allows her to live so well. I guess she still owns oil wells in east Texas somewhere. That's probably why Paul acts the way he does. He figures this is his house and his stuff. Sometimes Millie calls him "Mr. Daniels" out of respect.

There's another cat that I've seen only once or twice out of the corner of my eye, standing in a shadow or in a dark corner of an empty room. It's a sleek Siamese who howls at night, a really eerie, mournful sound. Millie says that he's just a stray who comes around occasionally and that he has no name. But there's more to it than that. I've seen her pet and cuddle him, talk to him in a language I don't understand. Mignon says that there's a town story that Millie was kidnapped by an Indian maharajah and had a love child who died. Really romantic and tragic at the same time. Maybe the Siamese is the maharajah. All I know is that cat is real mysterious—and he is the one subject Millie will not talk about.

As for the ghost, I've only seen her once, and believe me, once was enough. The really scary part is, at the time I saw her, I didn't even know she *was* a ghost.

Sometimes, on Fridays, Millie rents tapes from the local video shop and we make popcorn and settle into the plush cushions of the back parlor to watch old movies. Millie loves Bette Davis, Alfred Hitchcock, and some Swedish guy who makes really strange pictures. I like *Superfly*,

Denzel Washington, and anything with Sean Connery in it, but that's another story.

One Friday, I worked late at the diner because Jess had to go to Missoula. By the time I got home, it was eight o'clock, and my ass was dragging. Millie was already popping the popcorn and settling herself and the cats onto the couches.

"Juanita, is that you?"

She appeared in the front hall in a cloud of Joy perfume (her favorite, her second or third husband had loved it), pale pink satin robe, and matching slippers.

"Sorry I'm late. I had to cover for Jess . . ." Out of breath, I stepped out of the way as the mysterious Siamese entered silently behind me and disappeared into the dark dining room. Millie acted as if she hadn't see him.

"Never mind about *that*. I rented *Now Voyager* for tonight, and the popcorn is popping."

I groaned. I was really tired. And my feet hurt.

"Millie, I've been frying hamburgers all night, I smell like grease and onions. Let me take a shower first. Move, Antonio!"

Antonio gave me a hard look and a sniff, then turned on all four of his heels and stalked away.

Millie called after him in Italian, and I started up the stairs.

"Isn't Tonio going to watch the movie?"

Millie shook her head disgustedly and picked up Paul, who was trying to sneak out of the front door.

"He only likes Bertolucci and Rossellini. Hates American movies."

"Oh." The only Italian word I could pronounce was "spaghetti."

"Don't be too long, you don't want to miss the first part."

"I won't!" I called down.

The door to the "Blue Bathroom," which I shared with the absent Jewell Matthews, was closed, but I didn't think much of it since there was a family with several kids staying for the weekend, and they had probably run out of bathroom space. I went to my room, tore off my clothes, put on my robe, and grabbed my bath things. Then I headed down the hall. The bathroom door was now open and coming down the hall toward me was a dark-haired woman, carrying a basket. Her hair was long and loose, and she wore a flowing navy blue robe, kind of old-fashioned-looking.

"Hello," I said. At Millie's house, there were no strangers.

"Lovely evening, isn't it?" she responded as she passed. She smiled at me. There was the smell of roses in the air.

"Yes, it is," I agreed, and I went into the bathroom and closed the door. Before the door shut, I saw the woman turn the corner and climb the stairs to the third floor.

Later, when *Now Voyager* was on its closing credits and we were picking up the tissues we had dropped, I asked Millie about her weekend visitors.

"I see you're letting the weekenders use the Blue Bathroom," I told her as I removed a piece of popcorn from Louis's tail.

"The Blue Bathroom? Are you sure? I would have thought the two bathrooms in the Floral Suite would be enough."

I shrugged my shoulders, and moved to rewind the tape.

"Guess not. I met the mother coming out of the bathroom . . ." I paused a moment. "Are you sure you put them in the Floral Suite? She went upstairs." I tapped the Rewind button. Nothing happened. Shoot.

Millie turned around quickly and stared at me, her blue eyes narrowing.

"What did she look like?"

I looked closer at the VCR. No wonder nothing was happening. I was pressing the Stop button.

"Tall, thin with long, dark, stringy hair . . ."

"Navy blue flowing robe, carrying a basket?" Millie interrupted.

"Yeah, that's her," I said slowly. "How did you know?"

Millie grinned at me, and put a cigarette into her two-foot-long mother-of-pearl cigarette holder.

"No. That's not her. Ms. Archer is of medium height, stocky build, a tow-headed girl with freckles, walks like a football player."

"That's not who I saw."

"That's because *you* saw Elma Van Roan. You saw our ghost."

My fingers turned stiff and I felt a chill go through me. She had looked so real, not shadowy or luminous, not all white or spooky. I had spoken to a ghost? And stranger still, the ghost had spoken back.

"G-ghost?"

Millie's laughter sounded like little bells.

"You betcha! And if she was carrying that basket, she was headed up to the Tower Room to reenact the murder of her husband. Local legend says she carried the knives up to the room in a cloth-covered basket. Told her husband they were pastries," she said breezily.

I shivered and reached for the knitted afghan that Louis had burrowed into.

"M-murder? You . . . you never said a thing about a murder."

Millie's pretty face clouded for a moment as she tried to remember. "Oh . . . didn't I mention it?" she asked innocently. "It's a great story! Elma Van Roan found out that her husband, Fergus, was having an affair with the maid, a local girl. Elma and Fergus were just rooming here for a few months while their house was being built. Fergus was the Methodist minister."

I smiled despite my uneasiness. A minister. That figures.

"Elma spied them . . . ah . . . en flagrante, and decided to take matters into her own hands. She actually waited until morning, told her husband that she wanted to bring him a surprise for breakfast. Went to the kitchen and packed up the meat cleaver and a slicing knife into her basket. Went upstairs, gave her husband a muffin to eat, then cut off his . . . well . . . you can guess what she cut off. I'll bet *he* was surprised! She left him there to bleed to death and went after the maid. Elma was caught, of course, and hanged. Totally unrepentant. And she's never really left this house." She looked at me closely. "As you can attest."

By now I was shivering and shaking under the afghan as if it was twenty degrees below zero outside. I'd never met a ghost before. Especially one who was carrying knives.

"Ah . . . is she . . . ah . . . dangerous?" I asked. How stupid did that sound?

Millie smiled.

"No. Just wanders around the place. Speaks to the guests sometimes. Inez and I see her at least once a month. Occasionally, she ties up the bathroom, washing the blood off her hands, I think. She won't bother *you*. It's usually the male guests of the Tower Room who have trouble."

I didn't sleep well for a couple of nights after that. I

kept seeing the dark-haired woman carrying a basket up the stairs. A woman with an angelic smile on her face and the fury of hell in her heart.

But I was also having dreams of a different kind. The kind I hadn't had since I was fifteen, over a hundred years ago. And in all of them, I could see Jess Gardiner's face. And his quiet eyes.

Chapter Ten

Paper Moon is a spot in the road, with fifteen hundred people or so in the town and surrounding area. It's on the way to the Glacier National Park and Idaho, so a lot of people pass through in the spring, summer, and fall months. The antiques and craft shops stay open from April through September to accommodate the tourists. On weekends, the population swells. It's a big deal here. Reverend Hare told me proudly that Paper Moon had a traffic jam once last year in July.

But Paper Moon is, basically, a one-horse town. And most days it's kinda dead. It's just that no one has gotten around to burying it yet.

Most women could strip naked at the corner of Arcadia Lake Road and High Street and never draw a crowd.

But I bet you I could.

In a way, *I* became a sort of tourist attraction for Paper Moon. There were people of Scot, English, and Irish descent. Some with ancestors from Sweden and Norway, Ireland and Bavaria. There are Kootenai, Salish, Crow, and Cheyenne. There were Lakota, like Jess and his family, and Blackfoot. But there weren't many black *folk*.

Let me rephrase that.

There weren't *any* black folk.

I swore that some people came into the diner not just to eat but to look. At me. I told Jess I was thinking about selling tickets. He thought I was crazy.

I could spot them right away. They weren't even cool about it. They walk through the door, look around slowly, trying not to call attention to themselves. I knew what was going through their minds: "I don't see her. Where is she?" Then they would spot me, whisper to one another, and come on in. The whole time I'm cooking, or taking the orders from Mignon or Rosetta, I'd catch glimpses of them, looking at me, watching everything I did. Sometimes, when Jess rang up the bill on the register, they'd forget to take their change because they were watching me.

I told Jess, "This is starting to really piss me off."

"They just want to see we got diversity." He grinned.

I rolled my eyes and put a drop of vanilla in the batter.

"Aw, you're just seeing things," Jess told me, as he wiped up spilled milk and orange juice after a family of seven had departed. "You ain't that much of an oddity. We're so-phisticated, you know. We get colored folks around here all the time. Mignon," he called out, "didn't some black man pass through here with Lewis and Clark, back in 1804 or 1805? Somewhere back there?"

"Yeah, but he didn't stay, Jess," Mignon yelled back with a grin. "Said he wanted more of a cosmopolitan atmosphere."

I snickered at them, giving my pancake batter a stir for the nine o'clock rush.

"You call me colored again and we're gonna fight, Mr. Running Fox Gardiner," I told him, using his proper names. "I'm not just imagining things. Those people come in here just to stare at me."

"She's angling for a raise, Uncle Jess," Mignon commented. "Figures she's worth more since she thinks she's the main attraction, the one that customers are here to see."

"Hell, they're not here for her. They come for my Montana Continental French onion soup. And she won't get a raise," Jess retorted. "Besides, it's all in her head. Juanita's suffering from hormonal paranoia. Common for women of her age."

I threw a large rainbow trout at him.

But by eleven o'clock, I wasn't feeling any better. Five people had asked me about those "things" on my head— referring to the tiny, tight twists of hair I wore, which I kept out of my way by wrapping a cloth around my head like a headband.

Thank God my sister was a hairdresser!

Kay could do anything to anyone's hair—from bleached blondes to locks. And since I was her "little" sister, I had been her guinea pig ever since I had enough hair to comb. Any hairdo she had ever tried on my head (and there had been a million of them) she had taught me how to take care of myself. Including these twist things.

Good thing, too.

Francine's Beauty World in downtown Paper Moon, Montana, could do a mean wash and set but they didn't know a damn thing about my tightly coiled hair.

I was pissed off and getting tired of having to explain myself. Throwing the dishes around, slamming the pans down onto the stove. Jess came in the front door with Dracula. The place had quieted down—it was just before the lunch crowd came in. (We don't do "brunch" at the diner—it's breakfast, lunch, and dinner.)

"What's up with you?"

Dracula padded over to me and sat down, giving me a sad puppy-dog look. He wanted me to feel sorry for him so I would give him a piece of sausage.

"If one more person asks me what those 'things' are on my head, I'll knock 'im in *his* head with this frying pan!"

Jess shrugged, and poured himself some coffee.

"It's not their fault, Juanita. We don't get many African queens round here." His lips twisted upward into a smirk.

I looked at him out of the corner of my eye as I cleaned up the mess I had made, and handed Dracula his treat.

"I'm beginning to feel like an alien. Like I just landed here from Mars or somewhere."

"Something new and different, Your Highness."

"Hummph," I said, imitating his favorite word. "Well, *this* African queen is getting sick and tired of being a museum piece. Maybe I should tell 'em I'm practicing voodoo or something. That would give 'em something to talk about."

Jess stopped sipping for a moment. He was frowning.

"Is that like geechie?"

I turned and looked at him.

"Now where out here in the mountains of Montana did you ever hear about geechie?"

Jess shrugged his shoulders again and smiled that slight smile of his.

"My best friend in the army . . . was a black dude, Eddie

Rice. He was from South Carolina. Used to talk about this girl he was in love with. Said she was a 'geechie woman.' He told me he never crossed that girl, that she could mix up some potions that could mess him up good. Is that like voodoo?"

"I'd forgotten you were in the army," I told him. But I hadn't. Mignon said Jess had earned a Purple Heart. There were pictures of his regiment on the walls of the diner.

The glimmer in Jess's eye went out like a snap, and he got that distant, closed look he always gets when he doesn't want to talk about something.

"You and Eddie were tight, huh?" I asked, watching Jess, hoping that the door hadn't shut too tight.

"Yeah, he was the one who . . ." He stopped. In the silence, I heard the refrigerator hum.

"Yeah," he said with finality.

I knew why he had closed up.

I heard it in his voice. Knew it was there without even looking at his face. I just went on and put some bread in the toaster and added a pinch of sugar to my concoction. I wanted to keep the conversation as normal and boring as possible. I wanted to hear what he had to say about his buddy. I liked hearing the warmth and lightness in his voice. So I tried to be cool.

Nonchalant.

"Vietnam."

"Yep. Tunnel rat."

"Did Eddie get out?" But I knew the answer before I asked it. All of Jess's service stuff was arranged like a shrine on the mantel over the hearth in the diner. And in the middle of the "shrine" was a snapshot of Jess and a black guy, probably Eddie. Eddie hadn't made it.

"Blew up in front of my face."

I winced. My brother, Jerome, had died in a rice paddy near Saigon. There was barely enough of him left to bury. What they call a real "basket case." My mother never got over it. I turned back to the stove, but not before catching another good look at Jess's haunted face. Guess he had never gotten over it either.

I wanted to say something to him to make him feel better. I wanted to touch his shoulder and let him know that I understood. But I knew his memories were in a place I couldn't reach. And even if I could get there, he'd close the door in my face. I let it alone. I drank my coffee and said good-bye to some customers who were leaving.

I left Jess with his own thoughts and went back to the meat loaf I was making for lunch. Buried my hands in a bowl full of ground meat, egg, oatmeal, catsup, and spices. Squished it around a little, remembered that I needed to add more salt and pepper.

The idea struck me when I turned around and reached up to the shelf over the stove to get the salt box. It was the silliest thing. I laughed out loud and told Jess what I wanted to do.

Jess's eyes widened as I told him.

He shook his head firmly.

"No way! What're you gonna do? Run off all my customers? Forget it!"

I laughed and held up the cayenne pepper can and the bottle of cumin.

"Now, Jess, there are only a few things in this world that a little extra red pepper won't improve."

"What the hell . . ." he growled at me. "Juanita . . ."

"Or a little cumin . . . mixed with chili pepper . . ." I was on my tiptoes rummaging around the cabinet. There was another spice can that I couldn't quite reach.

"I wasn't planning on being sued for food poisoning, Juanita."

"You won't be. Besides, you'll be better off without those kind of customers, Jess. They deserve a little . . . there! Got it!"

Triumphantly, I held up the small jar of gumbo filé. "Just a little spice in their lives."

"Frankly, lady, you're enough spice . . . for all of us."

I sighed. I just loved it when he talked like that.

Jess's eyes locked with mine for a second then he looked more closely at the can I held in my hand.

"Christ! That's just what I need! Folks runnin' back 'n' forth to the can!"

He frowned a little and shook his head, his black hair spilling over his shoulders like an ebony waterfall. Asked a question, listened to my answer. Then he grinned at me.

"Juanita, you having hot flashes or what?" There was a twinkle in his eye.

I threw another trout at him.

But my idea came in handy a few weeks later. Especially on the day the Confederates arrived. But I'll get to that in a minute. Let me tell you about Millie.

I had the morning off. Rode with Millie over to Missoula for her doctor's appointment, and had just left her back at the rooming house. (The doctor said that Millie had the intestines of a twenty-year-old, but that's a story for another time and more information than I want to share.) It was a real experience driving on those two-lane roads in a 1961 white Cadillac convertible. Especially since Millie has a lead foot. My knees still get a little shaky when I think about it.

Millie insisted on driving (said it was Paul Daniels's car, and he wouldn't let anyone drive it but her) and drive she did—eighty-five-plus miles an hour both ways. I was a nervous wreck by the time we got back to Paper Moon.

She looked like Marilyn Monroe behind the wheel: huge, black sunglasses; a white scarf around her head, the ends tied behind; red lipstick; and just the tiniest hint of that blond hair peeking out from beneath the scarf. It was hard to believe that she was sixty-five, seventy, eighty, thirty, who knows?

"Millie, how old are you really?" I asked her breath-lessly. That last turn, taken at eighty miles an hour, had left my wind and my stomach behind.

Millie giggled.

"How old is the Sphinx? Nobody knows. If I tell you, you'll only gasp and say I look good for my age. Or, God forbid, you'll say I look 'well preserved.' Sounds like I'm a pickle. Let's just say I'm old enough to know better about most things, and young enough not to care too much."

The screeching of the tires brought a lump to my throat. Now, I'm a coffee-colored woman. If I blush, I have to let you know, because you can't see it on my face. But let me tell you something, after just fifteen minutes in the car with Millie, I was turning white, literally.

I saw the sheriff's car around the next bend. Thank the Lord, I thought, I am about to be delivered. Millie was go-ing to have to slow down, big time, if she didn't want to get a ticket. I settled back into the seat. But instead of slowing down, Millie floored the gas pedal and we flew past the patrol car like a jet on takeoff. The sheriff turned his lights and siren on, and came after us. I closed my eyes.

"Millie! Are you crazy? What are you doing?"

"Setting a record!" was the insane reply. And we sped down the road for a few miles, with the sheriff in hot pursuit.

Finally, Millie sighed deeply, stretched, and slowed the huge car down to a crawl, then pulled off the road and stopped. The patrol car pulled in front of us and turned off the siren. Millie lit a cigarette. She had a blissful, relaxed expression on her face. As if she'd just had sex.

I wanted to throw up.

The sheriff stalked over to the driver's side of the car, his ticket book in his hand. His face was stern, his eyes hidden behind reflective sunglasses. Millie exhaled loudly.

"License, please."

The officer didn't sound too happy. I wondered if Millie had been in trouble for speeding before.

Millie handed it over with a flourish. He barely glanced at it, then jotted something down on the ticket. He's gonna take her license away, I just know it, I said to myself.

Thank God.

"I clocked you at eighty-six miles an hour."

Millie blew a smoke ring but didn't say anything.

"You know what that means, don't you?" the sheriff asked, his voice clipped and unfriendly.

I know what it means, I thought. It means you're going to take her license away forever.

Millie blew out another smoke ring.

"Did I break the record?"

"Yes, ma'am," the officer acknowledged seriously. "And if you, Reverend Hare, and Mrs. Fitzpatrick ever make another bet like this, I'll haul all three of you in, do you understand me, Aunt Millie?"

Millie nodded, with a saucy tilt of her head. Blew out some more smoke.

The officer smiled, signed the ticket, and tore it off.

Aunt Millie?

"Well, at least it was a good cause. Reverend plans to use the money to supplement the food pantry," the officer remarked. "But Aunt Millie, you can't keep making bets like this, this has got to be the end of it! Seventy-five is one thing. But eighty-six is just plain crazy! You gotta keep the speed down. The next time we stop you, we'll have to take your license!" There was a note of earnestness and pleading in the man's voice. "Aunt Millie?"

Millie took the ticket and patted the concerned officer gently on the cheek.

"Juanita, my nephew, Horace Patterson, my sister Gertrude's baby boy. Isn't he a sweetie?" She crooned like she was talking to a two-year-old. "He was absolutely the most precious baby!" She slipped the ticket into her bosom. Horace Patterson blushed. "Horsey, this is Juanita Louis, the new chef at Jess's Diner."

"Glad to meet you, ma'am. I haven't had the pleasure yet of sampling your food, but I expect Diane and I will get to real soon. Mountain can't say enough about your French toast!"

Well, that was not a surprise. Mountain usually had four slices every morning, along with three eggs, hash browns, four sausage links, and three strips of bacon.

I thanked "Horsey" for the compliment, watched as Millie gave him a peck on the cheek and sent him on his way, just as if she was sending him off to kindergarten. He, in turn, again warned her against traveling over eighty miles an hour. Said it just wasn't safe. For the other drivers, that is.

"Aren't you afraid to drive so fast? What's the speed limit around here anyway?" I hadn't noticed a sign. 'Course, even if I *had*, we were traveling so fast, I wouldn't have been able to read it.

Millie grinned.

"Seventy-five, eighty, but who cares? Mountain Peters has emptied his ticket book on me more than once, and Horsey catches me now and then, but that's the fun of it. I see how fast I can go, he or one of the other sheriffs clock me, and we see if I've broken any records! My sister takes the bets."

"You're going to break more than that if you don't slow down," I growled at her.

"Don't be a spoilsport, Juanita, nobody's going to get hurt. We haven't passed a car for ten miles. And I started driving a car before your parents were born, used to drive Louis's car before the Grand Prix all the time. And no, I'm not afraid." She took both hands off the steering wheel to light another cigarette. I almost died right there. "Let me give you a piece of advice I've followed since I was sixteen years old. Whatever you are afraid to do, do it immediately. Taking risks will give you the best rewards in life. I've found that to be true without exception."

"Yeah, but you could also get killed." I gulped. I hadn't felt this bad since I took the kids on the Beast at Kings Island.

Millie shrugged.

"I could die tomorrow falling out of bed, or choking on a fish bone. Why not go out in a flash?" We hyper-spaced past a tired-looking Chevy that had crawled onto the highway. My life passed before my eyes. In review, it wasn't much.

"I'll pass if you don't mind," I told Millie. "I was plan-ning to pull my toenails out on Wednesday, and I'd hate to miss that."

Millie grinned and let her foot off the gas.

"OK, seventy-five, but not a bit less."

It was the best she could do.

"And remember, Juanita. Your fears can paralyze you. Always, but always, do what you're afraid to do. You'll be surprised to see how far it will take you."

By the time we got back to Paper Moon, I had barely recovered enough to walk without my legs shaking. Mil-lie parked the car in the garage and went inside to take a nap. She was hosting her bridge club that night. I mean-dered over to the diner on my way to the drugstore. I came in the back door since I wanted to check the supply of meat in the freezer. I'd place an order if we needed more. I peeked through the doors at the dining room but didn't notice anything unusual. Carl was at the counter. I didn't see Jess anywhere, but his truck was parked on the side so I figured he was probably in the back. A couple of locals sitting at table four; a table of eight giving their or-ders to Mignon; Fish Reynolds over in the corner reading the paper; and three red-faced good old boys at the coun-ter. At first, I didn't think much of that. Around here, red-faced good old boys are a dime a dozen.

But as I was to find out, these guys were different.

They were already a few sheets to the wind and it was only one-thirty. That usually meant trouble.

"Hey, Chief! Got any firewater? Ha, ha!"

"You all do rain dances anymore, kid?"

"Hey, why you cooking, anyway? I heard you got a *negro* cook now. A real tar baby. They moving west, now, huh? Ha, ha!"

I peeked out again. The boys were slapping each other on the back, real happy with the jokes they'd made. Mignon was at Mrs. Phelps's table, looking really nervous. Carl, who was carrying a tray filled with dirty dishes, had a dark, angry look on his face. When he went to the refrigerator, taking out hamburger patties, I heard them call him "Chief" again. I didn't hear what Carl said in reply. I got my tote bag and headed toward the ladies' room.

Normally, I probably would have just filled their orders, argued with 'em a bit, and left 'em alone. They were harmless, drunk but harmless. But today I felt like shaking things up bit—and them, too. Giving them a little nightmare they could only remember pieces of. And having some fun at their expense. Sometimes you have to be outrageous just to bring people back to what's real.

Besides, they were starting to piss me off.

"Yeah, I hear them blacks can cook, even if they can't do anything else except riot and rob people who got jobs and are hardworking. Good thing we don't have too many of 'em out here. That gal any good?"

"Boy, he's a wooden Injun, ain't he? Not much personality."

Carl's eyes widened when I came out of the back, but he didn't say anything. Just moved aside to let me take his place at the grill. Mignon almost dropped the plates she was carrying. Carl started grinning. I checked the progress of the hamburgers on the grill, lifted the fries out of the grease and shook them a little. It got so quiet in that place, you could have heard a mouse hiccup.

Jess came out of the back carrying a tray of salt and pepper shakers. He stopped in his tracks and his jaw dropped.

I know I was a sight.

I had wrapped my head cloth into a real fancy style a friend had shown me once. It stood almost a foot and a half high. I had a corncob pipe clenched in my teeth, and an amulet around my neck. The amulet wasn't an African piece, but Lakota, given to me by Jess's Aunt Portia, but these idiots wouldn't know the difference. With two arms full of bracelets jingling, I started chanting as I turned the burgers over.

The Good Old Boys weren't saying anything now, and I had my back to them, but I could feel them staring holes through me. I was looking forward to making them nervous. I reached up to the spice rack and picked up an old baby food jar that had an "X" on its label. Figured that ground meat might need a little more seasoning.

"Hey, what's that you putting on there?" Good Old Boy One had finally gotten the courage to speak.

I turned around and looked at him, letting my eyes talk, keeping my face still.

"My name is not 'Hey.' My name is Juanita. *Miss* Juanita to you." I continued to chant.

Carl stuck his fist into his mouth.

Good Old Boy One wasn't sure how to respond so he said nothing. Good Old Boy Two just laughed nervously.

Good Old Boy Three smirked and put his big, beefy elbows on my clean counter. I shook a little more of the "X"-marked spice on his burger, slapped a piece of cheese on top. Closed up the jar.

"Well, *Miss* Juanita, I don't want you putting no strange spices on my good old all-American hamburger. You hear?"

I picked up the cayenne pepper again and added a little extra. He was a big boy. It wouldn't kill him. Also pulled a little doll out of my apron pocket. Good Old Boy Two inhaled loudly. I stuck a pin in the doll's midsection. Good Old Boy One turned white. Good Old Boy Three's eyes got big. Behind their backs, Mignon, Mrs. Phelps, a family of tourists, and Reverend Hare were grinning.

Jess slapped Good Old Boy Three on the shoulder, shook him a little, too.

"Bobby, maybe that ain't such a good idea, talking like that. Miss Juanita here is real sensitive to those kind of things . . . and temperamental. Sort of takes things to heart, if you know what I mean." Jess leaned close. "I've heard that she practices . . ." I didn't hear the last part of that sentence. Jess continued: "Wouldn't do to piss her off. After all, she *is* cooking your hamburger."

I pushed the pin in a little farther, then set the doll, face-down, on the counter. Finished frying up those hamburgers.

Good Old Boy Three was quiet.

I set three cheeseburger platters with lettuce, tomato, onion, and extra fries on the counter in front of the three stooges. For a few seconds they just stared at those plates— and at me. I stared back. Puffed on my pipe (had borrowed some of Roy Porter's Cherry Blend tobacco) and picked up that little baby doll again and looked at it real close—pulled the pin in and out, in and out.

Good Old Boys One and Two just stared—eyes open

wide. Good Old Boy Three looked as if he was about to shit, or wind his watch, but he hadn't made up his mind yet.

"Ain't you boys gonna eat?" I asked, evenly. I locked eyes with Good Old Boy Three. His cheek twitched. "I fixed those burgers up special." I narrowed my eyes and blew a cloud of smoke out of the pipe right into his face. "Would hurt my feelings if you all didn't eat . . ." I let my voice trail off. Pushed that pin in—hard.

You never saw anybody eat hamburgers and fries so fast. Good Old Boy Three practically licked the plate clean—and all that extra gumbo filé that I'd sprinkled on it, too. He finished with a belch and a huge grin.

I was grinning, too. But I thought someone would have to carry Jess out. He was doubled over with laughter.

You see, gumbo filé is just ground-up sassafras leaves. You use a touch in Louisiana cooking, especially in gumbos and such. It gives the food a nice flavor, a little zing, and it thickens it a bit. Most people have had sassafras tea in their lives, your grandmomma probably gave it to you when you were little. Sassafras can be a bit like a laxative. A little bit is OK as a medicine.

But too much?

Well, I'd heard Good Old Boy Three say that he was headed down to Wyoming. He didn't know it yet, but it was going to be a long trip.

When he left, he said to me, "You know, I was just kidding. I kid Jess all the time, we're just like brothers. Me and the boys got started a little early today. Didn't mean nothing by it. Hope you didn't take it personally. By the way, I loved that hamburger."

I let my eyes, and my gumbo filé, answer him.

Mountain came in laughing a few days later. Put two huge elbows up on my counter.

"Hey, Juanita! Mignon!"

"Hi Mountain," Mignon spoke as she flew by with a tray full of food.

"Mountain! Didn't your momma teach you not to put your elbows on the table," I said, pouring him some coffee.

"Yes, ma'am. But I'm a slow learner," Mountain answered, grinning. "Got a little time today, Juanita. Give me a steak, three eggs, grits, a cinnamon roll, two pieces of toast, and a tall glass of orange juice."

"Coming up." I pulled a rib eye the size of Nebraska out of the refrigerator. "The orange juice is freshly squeezed today, Mountain," I added. I was in a pretty good mood.

"And I don't want whatever you gave Bobby Smith either." Mountain was still grinning.

"Bobby Smith?"

Mountain reached out to touch the sugar I had sprinkled on an apple pie cooling on the counter. I popped his hand.

"Ow!"

"Oh, quit! I didn't hurt you! But I will if you don't leave that pie alone. Who's Bobby Smith?"

Mountain pretended to pout. An interesting look for a WWF-sized state trooper.

"One of the boys who came by a few days ago. Remember? Three hamburgers, medium rare?"

I looked at him, put my hands on my hips. Pretended that my feelings were hurt.

"Now, Mountain, all I gave that boy was a cheeseburger, medium, extra fries, and a chocolate shake. Nothing unusual about that."

Mignon coughed, then cleared her throat.

Mountain downed the glass of orange juice in one gulp. Had an orange juice mustache on his top lip. He looked like a super-sized six-year-old.

"Yeah, sure," he said, laughing. "Whatever you say. Anyway, I'm headed toward Cheyenne on Fourteen. I see Bobby's green Ram parked by the side of the road. Nobody's in it. So I turn around, go back and park. Wonder if maybe Bobby's having engine trouble or something."

Mignon cleared her throat again.

"Mignon, you gotta sore throat or something?" I ask her, smiling as wide as I can smile.

"Oh, no, ma'am," she answered, exaggerating the "ma'am" part in her best fake Southern drawl. "Just a little tickle . . ." She grins. Coughs a little more.

"Well," Mountain continued, "I call out to old Bobby. You know, maybe he's hurt or met with some foul play. You remember, Mignon, we had problems with that pervert from Nevada last year this time. At first, I don't hear anything. Then I hear some scratching around, the bushes moving. And I hear somebody moan. I reach for my gun, call out to Bobby again.

" 'Mountain, is that you?' he yells from back in the bushes somewhere. I say, 'Bobby, it's me. Are you hurt or something?' He says no, he's not hurt, but do I have some. . . .' " I don't know if you've ever seen a seven-foot-tall, three-hundred-fifty-pound man blush before, but it's quite a sight. "Aw, excuse me, Juanita, Mignon. So Bobby says, 'Mountain, do you have any toilet paper?' And, of course, I'm always prepared, so I go get him some from out of my trunk. He tells me something he ate at the Paper Moon

Diner has run through him like Sherman through Georgia. Says he's had the shits, oh, excuse me, Juanita. I mean, he's had the diarrhea since Butte. Doesn't know what he's gonna do. I told him I eat at the Paper Moon practically every day, don't ever have any problems." Mountain reaches for a doughnut. Looks at me with twinkling, green eyes. "Bobby says I'd better be careful. Told me that the voodoo woman Jess has got cooking for him put a hex on the food, and that's what's making him sick." Mountain popped that doughnut in his mouth—all of it.

"Now, I told him there wasn't any voodoo woman working at the diner, just Juanita. He said 'Yeah, that's the one.' " Mountain chewed slowly, talking with his mouth full, then swallowed with one loud gulp. "Said the woman smoked a corncob pipe, wore a beaded headdress, and chanted while she flipped the burgers. Said she called herself 'Miss Juanita.' "

"Must have me mixed up with somebody else," I mumbled, tapping out a little black pepper on the steak.

Mountain looked at me sideways.

"You know any voodoo, Juanita?"

I smiled at Mountain. Handed him another doughnut.

"Noooo," I answered truthfully.

"So, what did you say then, Mountain?" Mignon asked as she put some toast down.

"I told Bobby that he needed to stop smoking that weed," said Mountain, chewing and smiling at the same time. "Told him he was imagining things, and it was giving him the shits, too. Oh, excuse me." In one sweeping movement, faster than I thought a man that size could move, Mountain scooped up the baby doll Carl's little sister had

loaned me. I had left it on the counter near the cake platter. He looked at it for a second, then set it down on the
stool beside him.

"I'm going past Route Three, Mignon," he said. "I'll drop
this off for Rowena, save you a trip." He gulped down the
second glass of orange juice I had poured him. Grinned at
me. "But you might want to take the pins out first, *Miss
Juanita.*"

Chapter Eleven

I came to Montana to see what's here. I picked Paper Moon because I liked the name—it reminded me of Teishia's laughter. I wanted to go west 'cause I figured it was opposite of where I'd come from. I wanted to hear the sound of birds instead of sirens, and see real animals, not just those poor, sluggish things you see in zoos. I wanted to walk along a lakeshore like they do in the movies. I left home to have an adventure: to do things I'd never done before.

But the truth was I became afraid that maybe I'd have to let some of these adventures go.

I was too scared.

I had been in Paper Moon over two months. I worked nine, ten hours a day at the diner. Came back to my room at Millie's and did my laundry, or helped Millie and Inez around the house. In the evenings, I watched television or just sat on the porch, read a book, scratched Louis behind the ears. Sometimes I would go into town, or ride over to

Mason with Jess to shop. Went to Missoula with Mignon last week. I walked to work along the highway, which followed the creek, but I hadn't walked along the lakeshore yet. There were some places I just wasn't brave enough to go.

The mountains rose behind the town, just beyond Arcadia Lake. I had never seen anything like them. Still haven't. They are beautiful, strange, awesome. Snowcapped in places. Even now.

The eagles screamed at each other over my head, and in my mind, they were calling me to follow them up to the mountain's top. Jess lives up there in a cabin on Kaylin's Ridge. Sometimes, early in the morning or late at night, I watched the smoke from his chimney weave its way through the huge pine trees, and then, as if freed from prison, it curled upward to the clouds. He'd asked me many times to walk up there with him. I would have loved to see it, I knew it was beautiful, but I was too scared to go.

Arcadia Lake sets at the bottom of the mountains, not far from the highway. I could see it from the back porch of the diner when I took my cigarette breaks. Through the curling, silver smoke, I saw its waters, dark yet clear. Early in the morning, the deer came through the trees to the shore to get a drink. The geese made an awful racket. There was a family of ducklings I liked to watch, especially the tiny one, who always got left behind.

The cool green of the pine trees along the shore tempted me, too. I wanted to walk along the water's edge, just to get my feet wet. Maybe sit on a rock and watch the deer, I wouldn't say anything. I just wanted to sit there. And listen to the quiet. God speaks in the quiet.

But I was too afraid. Would the trees crowd in on me? Would the mountains and the sky fall down on my head?

Mignon wanted me to go with her and her family to a powwow. All I knew about powwows came from old cowboy movies I'd seen on TV. I knew that wasn't right. But how many powwows did they have in Ohio? Mignon said it was like a big family reunion. I thought it might be fun. It was intertribal: people from different nations including Oglala Sioux like Jess and Mignon. They got together each year this time. The Two Trees Powwow is held back east, Mignon tells me. It's funny. When Mignon says "east," I think of Missouri or Illinois. She means Meagher County, Montana, a little south of Helena. I told her no, I have plans. But deep down I really wanted to go.

Mignon saw right through me.

"What plans?" she snorted. "You're gonna paint your toenails that weekend?"

"You're so smart." I pulled her braid. Mignon was becoming like a daughter to me; I helped her with her little boyfriend problems; she sassed me just for fun.

"For your information, Miss Thang, since this place will be closed, I thought I'd go up to Kalispell, maybe see the park, too."

Mignon shook her head. "I don't believe it. You won't walk half a mile with me to Jess's cabin over on Kaylin's Ridge. And you're going to Glacier National Park? By yourself? Not likely."

"Well, I'm going," I told her testily. I was mad at her for not believing my lie.

"And *I* don't buy it, girlfriend," she shot back as she went off to deliver a tray of food.

"Tough titty," I said, under my breath. I turned back to

the pork and beans I was fixing to put in the oven. She had some nerve. I didn't want to hurt Mignon's feelings. Her family had been nice to me. Along with Millie, and most of the other folks in town, they made life pleasant here for me, considering that I was a total stranger. And Jess had given me a job.

But I was too embarrassed to tell them that I was afraid to walk along the lake, or climb up the ridge to Jess's cabin, or go fishing with Abel and the boys, or sit on a plain in the middle of the big sky.

Two Trees Plain is near the foothills of the Rockies. It's a wide-open place, and I'm afraid of wide-open places. How stupid is that? I'm scared that all that air will close in on me, afraid that the mountains will fall down on me, and make me crouch on the ground, curl into a little ball and cry.

I'm afraid of the emptiness of the plain, where God stretches out forever, and I will have no place to hide.

I have spent my whole life in close, cramped, noisy spaces with people falling on top of each other. Crowded cages, really. Tiny apartments, buses, the halls of the hospital, its closet-sized rooms. And as much as I love it here, when you take me away from the cage, I don't know which way to go, or what to do.

It has taken me almost a month to get used to the quiet nights. There are no sirens or loud cursing to lull me to sleep. No gunshots to make me sit up straight in bed at three A.M., about to have a heart attack, hoping Rashawn and Bertie are in for the night, that little Teishia isn't the victim of a drive-by.

The birds sing and cackle, and early in the morning I hear Riddle's Creek gurgling behind Millie's house. When

I'm in the house, or standing on the back porch of the diner, I feel safe. The animal sounds can't get me. The quiet won't force me to lose myself in my thoughts. But if I go out there, out in the open, where there's only trees or open space or mountains and real earth beneath my feet, who's to say? I have no history with open spaces or mountains or lakes. In such a place, like the Two Trees Plain, where there is nothing to hide you, there are no excuses. The plain seems endless. The mountains kiss the sky. There are no windows you can shut.

Jess closed the diner after the breakfast rush on Friday, and spent the next few hours loading up the truck. Mignon's family went over early. Mary, Jess's sister, had a tent to set up and food to cook. Her husband, Raymond, and Mignon and Carl had gone with her. I pretended that I had things to do. Made sure the diner was spick-and-span. We wouldn't be open again until Monday. Mopped and waxed all the floors, cleaned out that sparkling oven. Made sure I had dusted away every speck of nonexistent dust. Did a good job of making work for myself. Finally, I just gave up, gathered my things, and headed out the door. Jess and Dracula pulled up with a screech of tires just as I turned the key in the lock.

Jess sat there looking at me for a few seconds before he spoke.

"You missed your bus to Kalispell."

I glared at him, kept walking.

"I'm taking the next one."

His lips curled up in a smirk. He had on those reflective sunglasses that I hated.

"Ain't no next one, African Queen."

"So I'll take the nine-thirty tomorrow, Lakota Man," I

snapped back. I came down the steps and headed toward the road, and Millie's.

"I just love it when you talk that way," he teased me, grinning. "Come on, Juanita. Get in. I'll run you over to Millie's."

"No, thanks. It's only a short walk."

"No problem," Jess grunted back. He opened the door to the truck. "Get in."

I rolled my eyes.

"I'll walk."

"Well, that's the thanks I get for trying to be a gentleman. Offer the lady a ride, she snaps my head off."

I stopped and looked at him.

Jess grinned. Elbowed Dracula, and patted the seat next to him.

"Well, since you're going to make a fuss." I climbed into the cab. Pushed Dracula over. He whined and begged to be scratched.

Jess screeched away, leaving a cloud of dust behind us, roared down Arcadia Lake Road, then turned onto I-90 and took off. I was being kidnapped.

"This is not the way to Millie's," I said, mentioning the obvious.

Jess shrugged his shoulders.

"Thought I'd take a detour."

"A detour through where? Wyoming?"

"Oughta be in Two Trees in three, four hours. Then I'll take you back to Millie's."

"When?"

"Sunday night."

"Sunday *night?*" I should have known. "I can't go to Two Trees! I was planning on going up to the park! And besides, I don't have any clothes! I didn't bring anything! All of my stuff is at Millie's!"

Jess was unfazed. He smiled at me. I was hot. Well, sort of.

"You're about Mary's size," he said, referring to his sister. "You can borrow some of her clothes."

"Nice of you to offer," I said, sarcastically. "But I don't have a toothbrush . . . or a comb . . ." A stupid thing to say since I had all these twists in my hair.

Jess looked at the top of my head, and grinned. His whole face was turned upward with his smile.

"Juanita, they sell toothbrushes all over the country. Even in Two Trees, Montana. And as for a comb . . ." He made a face and pulled one of my corkscrews of hair. I swatted at his hand.

I wished I had a trout to hit him with.

"This is kidnapping, you know," I said, trying to act upset. I wiped Dracula's slobber off my jeans. In about four thousand years, I might get used to that dog's slobber.

Jess was not intimidated.

He laughed.

"Yeah. Ain't it?"

At Two Trees, Mignon, Carl, and Mary weren't surprised to see me. Mary handed me an apron and a spoon, told me she couldn't remember my recipe for buffalo wings and to hop to it. Said we'd have fifty hungry relatives to feed in a few hours. Mignon saw me and smiled that smile. Said she just happened to have an extra sleeping bag and pillow with her. Mary pointed out a tote bag full of *my* clothes. I was not fooled.

We ate, and I met every Gardiner relative west of the Missouri River. Although I caught some sideways looks

(Jess says I'm the only African American queen for miles), everyone was warm and friendly. And they wouldn't stop feeding me. I ate so much, I was miserable.

But the plains made me nervous.

I stayed close to Mary and Mignon, and close to camp. The plains opened up on the east, the land stretching out flat and smooth for miles. And to the north, I could see the Rocky Mountains. There was nowhere to hide. It made my stomach jumpy.

So I kept to the small places.

The next morning I cooked breakfast for fifty people— the entire clan. I was so busy, I didn't notice the activity going on at the west campground. By the time I got breakfast cooked and served, there were those who were ready for lunch. It was one-thirty before one of Jess's female cousins took over and I headed back to Mary's trailer to lie down.

Just as I reached for the door handle, the drums started.

And I stopped to feel them.

When my daughter Bertie was in middle school and still listening to what I told her, she joined a little dance group that met after school in the auditorium. Bertie loved that class. They learned ballet, you know, dancing on your tippy toes. They learned modern dances with scarves and poles, and Irish folk dances (although I never could figure out why little black kids on the east side needed to know Irish folk dances. Did they teach African dance to the little Irish kids in the all-white suburbs of the city?).

After six weeks or so, they had a recital. The teacher and the students painted the sets, and made the costumes and props themselves. Those little girls were so proud.

They danced to Tchaikovsky and to Duke Ellington's

"Satin Doll." They tap-danced with cardboard top hats, and pretended they were cats in *The Pink Panther*.

And then the drums started.

Bertie and the other girls swayed back and forth to the intensity of the sound, then broke into a traditional West African dance. By the time the girls finished, we were all on our feet.

But it wasn't so much the dance we were responding to as the drums.

Now, like then, I felt the drums before I heard them.

The pounding rhythm caught up with my pulse and pulled it along to a faster beat. The blood raced through my veins to catch up, and my body began to move. The constant "tom, tom, tom" pulled at my guts and echoed deep into my bowels.

I ran over to join Mignon and Mary in the crowd, and watched as the men and boys I had served buffalo wings and hamburgers to yesterday afternoon danced.

I did not recognize them.

The cowboy hats, jeans, denim shirts, and lizard-skin boots had all gone. So had the wire-rimmed glasses, watches, and silver belt buckles. There were no Ray-Bans or Nike Air Jordan sneakers to be seen.

Their faces were painted, red and white on the cheek, and the work shirts had been replaced by bare skin or fawn-colored animal skins trimmed with feathers and multi-colored beads. There was turquoise everywhere, and some of the clothes were marked with symbols I had never seen before.

The drummers sang and chanted, using words I did not understand. Their voices were high and screeching some-times, low and almost mournful other times. The drums kept time. The syllables were foreign to me, but the meaning, somehow, got through.

I picked Jess and Carl out of the group, but just barely. The drums had changed them. They were other people now, strangers, living in another place and time. They were dancing for a dream long gone, or one yet to come.

They kept pace with the drum, lifting their knees high, bobbing their heads up and down. Jess's eyes were closed. His lips moved as if he were praying to himself. I wondered what he was thinking about. I wondered if he was thinking at all.

As I watched, the whole scene became hazy and strange, sort of like I was looking at the dancers through an old nylon stocking or something. Like a dream.

Real, but not real. And it touched me deep, in a place I can't describe in words.

It was like church. Sometimes, when you listen to the preacher, and something he says touches you, you feel hot tears slipping through the corners of your eyes. And your throat gets tight. Or when the hymn is especially great, and the joy in your heart overcomes you with reverence and pleasure. And you shout "Amen!"

That was what it was like.

Like religion. It was no wonder that Jess was not himself. He had got the spirit.

I had got it, too.

Got up real early the next day, washed up, and threw on some clothes. Put on the coffeepot, and left Mignon sleeping, buried under the quilts. Headed for the nearest Porta-Potty, but noticed it was way 'cross the campground, and I had to pee bad. So I decided to take my chances with nature. Grabbed the toilet paper and headed out toward the plains. Scared up some rabbits and a snake, as Abel would say. Scared myself, too.

Watched the sun come all the way up, and put my hand up to my forehead to see if I could see as far as Minnesota. That's what Jess had said about this place. "It's so flat that, on a clear day, you can see all the way to Minnesota." Well, it was a clear day, and I could see far, but since I didn't know what Minnesota looked like, I wasn't sure if I saw it or not.

I turned to go back and had walked a little ways, too, before I realized that I was lost. An eagle flew over and screeched. I jumped and my blood ran cold. Stopped and went back the way I thought I came. But that wasn't right either.

The plains stretched out forever in front of me, and I could see good enough. I could see that there were no tents, trailers, or trucks. No campfires, no stalls, no people. There was nothing but land, a few boulders and some scruffy little bushes.

My heart pounded in my chest and my ears, and I kept repeating to myself over and over, "Be cool, don't get upset, you're only a few steps away from camp," but it didn't work. My stomach started quivering when I turned the opposite way and found myself staring into a solid wall of green pine trees that led up into the mountains.

I twirled around again and tried to go back over my steps. Looked for the rock where I'd set the toilet paper. Searched and searched for the little rabbit hole I'd stumbled over, the skinny little bush I'd seen with its tiny purple flowers.

Instead, I felt the wall of green begin to close in on me from behind, while the huge, open sky began to drop onto my head. And while I wanted to run toward the open plains to get away, where would I go? What was out there?

So I let the sky push me down onto the ground until I was curled into a little ball, shaking like a leaf and staring at the wall of green that seemed to be moving in my direction.

"Juanita! Juanita! Where are you? Juanita!"

I could barely hear his voice because my heart was pounding in my ears. I felt him before I saw him, because I had closed my eyes against the huge moving green wall that was threatening to swallow me up.

"Juanita! My God, what's the matter? What's happened?"

He covered me with his body, and gently uncurled my shoulders with his hands, pulling me to my feet, then supporting me when my shaking knees buckled.

"Jesus Christ, Juanita! Where the hell have you been? What happened to you? Did a bear attack?" He looked wildly around us, scanning the landscape with a trained eye for telltale signs of his brother bear.

"N-n-no." I could barely talk with my teeth chattering. "I-I went to pee an-and got l-lost."

He pulled me close and chuckled. I could feel his chest rise and fall with his laughter. I was too scared to get mad.

"Woman, you were never lost. We're about two hundred yards away from camp." He pointed. "That way."

"I-I-I'm scared of-of places like this . . . open, wild p-places," I stuttered out, tears streaming down my face.

Jess chuckled again. If I'd been in my kitchen at the diner, I'd have thrown a steak or a wooden spoon or something at him for laughing at me. But I was so glad that he was here, I could put up with a few chuckles at my expense.

"Montana ain't the place to be agoraphobic," he said, laughing.

"A-a-gora . . ."

"Agoraphobic," Jess repeated, gently wiping the tears from my cheek. Stroking my hair. "It means that you're afraid of being in open places."

"Oh." I was still shaking a little, but I wasn't stuttering anymore. I liked having my cheek stroked, my hair touched by a gentle hand. "Guess I'd better get over it. It's just that . . . that I ain't never been nowhere like this before. This big place, all this open space. I always lived in small, tight places, with walls you could see." I shivered a little. Jess's arm tightened around my shoulders.

"We all got demons riding us, Miss Juanita. You get over 'em or not. And you're either in a good or bad place to get over yours." Jess reached up to touch my twists again, then looked at me, blushed a little, and grabbed my arm instead. "Come on, let's get back. Mary's looking for an idiot to help her cook breakfast for fifty people." He grinned slyly. "That's why I'm here. She told me to come and get you."

I didn't have a trout or a wooden spoon, so I pulled my head scarf off and swatted at him with it.

Chapter Twelve

When Jess told me that we all have demons riding us at one time or other in our lives, I thought he was talking about me. Trying to help me get over being scared of the plains and the forest and things. But he was really talking about himself. I didn't know it then but he had a demon sitting on his shoulders, too. And Jess's demon was taller than a high-rise, wider than the Mississippi River, and deeper than the blue sea. His demon was slippery as a piece of cooked spaghetti, meaner than a black snake and twice as vicious. I stumbled over that demon with both feet. And it got angry with me, reared its ugly head, and tried to bite me. But I didn't let it kick my ass.

And it all started with Inez's pecan pie.

It's one of the few things in this world that I can't make. My sister Kay makes a delicious one, but every time I try, I end up with brown goo in a pie shell that looks like toxic waste and nobody will eat it.

But I love pecan pie.

And Millie's housekeeper, Inez, makes a great one. So after dinner on Thursday, I had two, good-sized pieces. With whipped cream on top. And chocolate shavings. And served with a dessert wine.

I had gas and a stomachache all night. Popped Tums like they were candy. Finally fell asleep at three-thirty. Had the alarm set for five so I could open the diner, but I overslept until six-thirty. I threw myself together in ten minutes and ran over to the diner, only to get tackled by Dracula when I opened the door.

I gave him his Dog Chow with a spoonful of Pedigree on top. He tackled me again and tried to lick my neck. I swatted him away. My stomach quivered.

"Dracula, honey," I pushed him away. "Today, I just ain't in the mood."

Abel and the boys were sitting on the front porch, grumbling and wondering where I was at and what was taking me so long.

I barely got a chance at eight-thirty to take an Alka-Seltzer before a tour bus called up asking could they stop for breakfast. With fifty-three people.

From nine on it was nonstop through lunch. It didn't let up until almost two, and I was dead by then. Couldn't wait to get off my feet and onto the couch in Millie's back parlor, where I could nurse my gassy stomach with some chamomile tea.

That was when Mary told me it was "E-Day."

Let me back up a bit. First, she told me I'd have to work for Jess that night. Spend eight more hours in front of a stove. On my feet. Cooking those unpronounceable dishes Jess created for dinner.

"No, and not just no. Hell no. My stomach won't let me," I growled at Mary. I was a real bitch that day.

"Please, Juanita. At least you can cook the venison steaks. I'll make the sauce. I'm desperate!" Mary pleaded with me.

"And *I'm* sick, Mary, and tired. Besides, where is Wonder Chef, anyway? Why isn't he coming in today? Is he sick?"

"No, he's drunk," Mignon said matter-of-factly as she flew past with a tray filled with apple and rhubarb pie and ice cream sundaes.

"Drunk?" I didn't believe it. I'd never even seen Jess sip a beer.

"Mignon!" Mary chided her daughter, her cheeks coloring.

"It's E-Day," Mignon continued, her voice flat with disgust. "He always gets drunk on E-Day."

"E-Day?" Now I was confused. "Is that like D-Day?"

Mary chuckled bitterly.

"Not exactly." She pointed toward the hearth where Jess's Vietnam memorabilia was on display. "E is for Eddie. Eddie Rice was Jess's best friend in the army. In Vietnam, Eddie told Jess to get behind him when they crossed a marsh near Da Nang. He stepped on a mine. If Eddie hadn't been there . . . Jess would be dead, too."

"But Jess blames himself for not going first," Mignon commented, dryly. "Blames himself for not dying, too."

Mary looked at her daughter with an evil eye but didn't say anything.

"So at regular intervals, Uncle Jess gets plastered. As punishment, I guess. For not dying." Mignon shook her head, her braids flying back and forth. "Don't ask me to explain it, I don't really get it, anyway."

"Sounds to me like you're doing fine," Mary snapped. Mignon shrugged her shoulders, and disappeared into the back.

"Regular intervals?" I tried to think. Jess had been here practically every day for the past three months. And he'd never been drunk as far as I remembered. Not even tipsy. "What's a regular interval?"

Mary shrugged.

"Well, before you came, it was once or twice a month, and definitely on Veterans Day, the Fourth of July, Memorial Day, and Eddie Rice's birthday. You came before the Fourth, and Jess was OK . . ." She frowned as she arranged silverware on a tray and sighed. "I guess he's making up for missing a day."

I looked at the picture of Jess and Eddie Rice. Saw the way they grinned into the camera. Noticed the pride in their tired young faces. The strength in their dark eyes. I thought about my brother, Jerome. God, they were just babies.

Then my stomach grumbled.

Now, normally, whenever anybody talks about Vietnam, I get sad and thoughtful. I get real sympathetic. My brother went over there tall and strong, not happy about going, but determined to do a good job. And come home. He came back in a flag-draped coffin. Jerome left a wife and a little baby. Lots of my brother's friends served there, too, so I have strong memories of that time and of that place, even though I've never been there myself.

But that's normally.

Today, I had a stomachache, a headache, and was getting my period. I was tired. And evil. And the thought of spending eight more hours on my feet covering for Jess, who was home drunk—regardless of the reason—was not my idea of fun.

I pulled my apron off, threw it down, and headed for the door.

Mary and Mignon stared at me.

"Where are you going?"

"Going to get Jess. I'll be damned if I'm working tonight, too!"

I heard some heavy breathing behind me. I looked over my shoulder. Dracula was there looking at me hopefully.

I pointed in the opposite direction.

"Beat it."

I marched down the steps of the diner and let the door slam behind me. Stalked out of the parking lot and onto the highway. Waved to one of Carl's friends who was driving down the mountain on a motorcycle, and waved at the girl who works in the carry-out at the gas station. As I walked along the highway, I noticed a few more trucks than usual, and was glad that I'd defrosted those extra steaks this morning. Hoped that Mary would remember to stir the chili from the bottom.

Arcadia Lake Road winds its way past the diner and around the lake. It also meanders up the mountain to Kaylin's Ridge, and that was just where I was headed. The higher I climbed, the cooler and lighter the air became. The cooler and lighter the air was, the better I felt.

The road dead-ends at the top of the ridge. I swatted at the decrepit mailbox half standing, half leaning next to an old maple tree. You could hardly see the name: "J. Gardiner." I turned down the gravel road that led to Jess's place.

There was sunlight here and there, peeking through the trees. The forest surrounded me with cool, greenness, and sweet smells that soothed my sore stomach. The gravel crunched under my feet, the sounds sending little furry creatures that I could not see, but could hear, scampering off into the darkness. I smiled. This place reminded me of the enchanted forest where Dorothy met the Cowardly Lion. The road was steep and muddy in some places, but not too tough to climb. When I reached the crest of the ridge, I stopped to catch my breath. And to see.

Down below me was Arcadia Lake, blue-green and beautiful, like a precious stone, sparkling in the sunlight, with the lake road winding around it like a silk ribbon. I saw the roof of the diner and watched as a red car turned into the parking lot. A convoy of four semis turned in behind it. A twig snapped and I looked to my left. A doe passed through the trees below me on the ridge. She stopped and looked around. I held my breath. She seemed to look at me for a moment, then decided that I wasn't worth more attention, and strolled away. I chuckled to myself.

Jess's cabin looks like something from the old days: rough and rustic, made completely out of logs. Just like Lincoln Logs, everything was dark brown but the door, which was painted bright green. The shades were drawn, and the curtains had been pulled closed. I listened for a second. There was no sound at all besides the sound of the forest around me. The peace sounded beautiful. I sighed, and balled my hands up into two fists. Knocked on that door like the big bad wolf.

At first, I didn't hear anything. Then I knocked again. Harder. Louder. And started yelling out Jess's name, too.

"Who the hell is it?"

"It's Juanita. Open the door!"

"No!"

"Open the door, Jess!"

"Fuck you!"

"In your dreams!"

"Go away!" came a rough, evil voice from inside.

"No," came my rough, evil voice from outside.

"Go away, damn you!"

"Don't you curse at me, asshole!" I pounded on the door even harder. My knuckles were getting sore. "Now open this door!"

"Shit!" came a loud hiss from inside.

The door opened. Jess looked out at me with two very black, very bloodshot, and very mean-looking eyes.

"All right. The door's open. Now what do you want?"

"I want to know when you're coming to work today. I want to tell you that I ain't covering for your sorry ass just because you decided it was a holiday and got tore up. That's what the hell I want."

"Go 'way, J'nita." He pushed the door toward me, but I stopped it with my hand.

"If you think I'm gonna cover for your tired behind tonight, you're making a royal mistake. I've worked my shift. I've got gas and a stomachache" (although both were miraculously gone now) "and I don't feel like working eight more hours while you sit up here like the hermit on the hill and feel sorry for yourself."

"Go 'way, 'Nita. Mary will take care o' things."

"Yeah, well, I've a good mind to tell her to go home. It's not fair to her either." I studied him for a second. "And it's *Juanita* to you."

You never saw a sorrier creation. His hair was damp and stringy, his face long and drawn, and his clothes were wrinkled up and stained.

And he stank to high heaven.

"You look like a tale from the crypt."

"Look, this doesn't kasern you. I'll talk to Mary," Jess said evilly, narrowing his eyes, and moving to close the door in my face again.

"Yeah, it does," I snapped back, pushing the door open. " 'Cause you on *my* time now."

Jess looked at me again. Tried to narrow one eye, and got dizzy. Almost fell down.

"What you mean, your time?"

"Whose time did you think it was? You think every month or so, it's OK to get drunk out of your mind, have an out-of-body experience . . . and leave all the dirty work *and* the worry on Mary? Well, that shit may have worked a few months ago, but now you dealing with *me*. And I ain't taking up your slack, Jess Gardiner. Especially not today."

"Oh? What's so special 'bout t'day?" Jess growled, trying to keep his balance.

"I got cramps."

He groaned and looked like he was going to throw up.

I grinned. Men get queasy when you start talking about periods and cramps and things. I love it.

He leaned against the doorjamb and closed his eyes. I've been drunk before, I know what it's like. I knew he was trying to get the room to stop spinning and his stomach to settle down. At first I thought he was going to pass out, 'cause his face went pale on me, but then he took a deep breath and opened his eyes. They were filled with tears. Then he gave me a look that could break a heart of concrete.

"You don't know how it *was*, Juanita," he choked out.

"No, baby, I don't. I can only imagine," I whispered. Wanting to cry myself. Wanting to stroke his hair, and squeeze his shoulder. "I know it was hot and wet there . . . and dangerous. I know you spent twenty-four out of twenty-four hours a day scared shitless, and wondering if you'd ever see the plains of Montana again. I know . . ."

A line from one of my brother Jerome's last letters to my momma jumped into my head. I was only fifteen when he wrote it, and too young then to understand what he meant. But I understood now.

Jerome had written:

"Momma, sometimes I have to see things, do things I don't want to see, don't want to do. I got to follow orders. I got to do what the man say. Awful things I can't talk about. But Momma, I think God he make me burn in hell for this. And I don't sleep too good thinking about that. Dream about all the things I done. I don't want to go to hell, Momma. So I split myself in two parts, that part that do things and see things no person should, and the other part that just scared to death and don't see nothing, don't remember nothing, and trying to live long enough to come home. The part that can forget."

"Only problem is you can't forget," Jess whispered. "No matter how many parts there are, none of them can forget."

Jess just stared at something in front of me. The strength of his memory was so strong that I could see it and smell the damp southeast Asian jungle, the acrid na-palm, and the peppery stench of gunpowder. I saw past

the curtain of the deep foliage of the rain forest into a
marsh filled with mines.

"Every night when I sleep, I see him. I see Eddie walking in front of me. Pushing me back with one strong arm.
Motioning for me to be silent. And then moving forward
maybe fifteen, twenty feet and then . . . he's gone." He
stared into space and I knew that he was watching Eddie
die again. "No screams. No crying. Just gone."

I closed my eyes.

Just gone.

"Maybe you need to quit trying," I said.

"Quit trying what?"

"Quit trying to forget."

"I got to forget or I can't sleep, I can't eat . . ."

"Who says you got to forget? Maybe that's what's
wrong. Maybe that's what was tearing my brother apart.
Maybe that's what's tearing *you* apart. Half of you is trying
to remember. And half of you is trying to forget. And
they're fighting each other. Just like in the war. Don't
worry 'bout gettin' over it, you just have to get on with it."

His head was down and a ray of sunlight sneaked
through a crack in the blinds, and made the silver in his
hair sparkle like new snow in the sun. It was so pretty I
reached out and stroked it gently. Jess looked up at me
with the strangest look on his face. I pulled my hand back
quick.

"Maybe you need to quit trying to fight yourself, Jess.
Quit trying to forget about Vietnam, and everything you
saw and . . . and did. And Eddie." Was I saying this right?
I knew what I meant, but was I telling him what I felt in
my heart? "Maybe you just need to let yourself remember.

And let it go." His eyes flooded over. And mine did, too. "Maybe it's OK to remember. No matter how awful it was."

I stopped then. I didn't know what else to say. I didn't know if what I had said was the right thing or not. I just looked at Jess. And he looked at me. Then he reached up and stroked my hair, the coils on the side, where I got some gray that Kay didn't color yet. And he smiled a little. A small, sick-looking but sweet crooked little smile. And he said, "Wait for me. I'll be right back."

I waited. Got a tissue and dabbed my eyes and blew my nose. And watched the hawks fly.

When Jess came out of the bathroom, he was cleaner than the board of health, but his face looked like something an old cat had been dragging around for a few weeks. Actually, he looked green. Maybe this hadn't been such a good idea.

He followed me out of the cabin without hardly saying anything, then locked the door. I walked to the end of the porch and looked out over the ravine and down the mountain to where the lake glistened in the sunlight. Beautiful.

"Juanita? Juanita?"

I turned to look at Jess.

"What?"

He was frowning at me. Looking out into the driveway where his truck sat by itself.

"How did you get up here? Did Mignon drive you?"

"No, she has class today. I . . ."

I stopped. And looked around. I was surrounded by trees and woods, by little furry animals and big furry animals, by eagles and butterflies, by huge pine trees. I was deep in a Montana forest, up on a small mountain ridge. I had walked here.

And I hadn't been afraid. I had been so mad at Jess for making me work extra hours, so pissed off that Mary was going to cover for him, that I had stormed up this mountain on foot, by myself, without blinking an eye or giving myself time to get scared.

And I wasn't scared now either.

"I walked up," I told Jess proudly as if it was something I did every day.

He looked at me for a moment. Narrowed those eyes again. I narrowed mine back.

"You know," I said nonchalantly, "a friend told me once that everyone has demons riding their backs from time to time. You get over them or not." I shrugged my shoulders. "I've heard that Montana is about as good a place as any to do that, though."

Jess was silent.

That night, the Paper Moon Diner had a new entree on the menu. "Venison steak with sauce Juanita," described by the chef as a delicate little basil-flavored cream sauce with strong character.

It was good, too.

Chapter Thirteen

I gave Peaches Bradshaw a big hug and a kiss on the cheek when she came into the Paper Moon Diner one hot Wednesday morning almost ten weeks to the day after she had dropped me off. This caused a little excitement since everyone round here knows that Peaches is gay, and they've not really seen me with any men since I've been here. I let them think what they wanted. Jess's eyebrow raised a little but I ignored him, too. He should know better. Peaches is a friend, and besides, she practically saved my life by bringing me here.

I fried her up some eggs and bacon, poured a tall glass of orange juice, and threw on some buttermilk biscuits. Gave the spatula to Jess, who was on the phone, while I sat down with Peaches, ignoring the veiled stares of Dr. Reid and Mr. Ohlson.

"When I dropped you off in the parking lot, I thought you would come here to get something to eat, not to take over!" she exclaimed after I told her about my life in Paper

Moon. "I can't believe Jess let you change the menu that way. He was determined to make this a gourmet's paradise!"

Jess was looking at us, the phone still clapped against his ear. He waved. Peaches waved back.

"The gourmetts weren't payin' the bills," I told her, deliberately mispronouncing the word. "Besides, he can still whip up his Continental concoctions. He's even teaching me some of his recipes, although I think most of that stuff is just meat with a sauce and weeds on the side."

"You've done wonders for this place," she said, looking around at the breakfast crowd. "Business looks good. Jess has gotta be happy about it."

I glanced over at him, flipping the pancakes the way I had taught him. But he was flipping them one-handed. The telephone receiver was still scrunched between his shoulder and his ear. I wondered who he was talking to.

"Hard to tell. He is not the most excitable person in the world."

Peaches narrowed her eyes for a second but she didn't say anything. Then she stabbed at another piece of bacon and popped it into her mouth.

She laughed when I told her about the good old boys, "Miss Juanita," and Millie's cats. And she wanted to know all about my encounter with the ghost. Peaches is into the paranormal.

"She actually *spoke*? You could hear her?" Peaches asked with her mouth full. "Was her voice full of echoes and static? Or was it clear and plain?"

"As plain as I hear you. Well, a little plainer, really. She smiled at me. I even smelled her perfume. It was like roses."

"Amazing."

"She was as real as you are. I thought Millie was kidding

when she told me that I had just spoke to . . . a ghost." I shivered a little. Even now, the thought of Elma Van Roan wandering the halls of Millie's house gave me the chills.

"Unbelievable."

"And did you know that Millie has a Siamese cat? One she talks to only in a foreign language? She won't tell me his name. He runs away whenever anyone else comes into the room. It's strange."

"Millie's strange. There's been a rumor round here for ages that she keeps a mentally disturbed child in one of her rooms. Wilma Ewings, the hairdresser over in Mason? She bleaches Millie's hair. She says Millie told her once that she had a child, but it was so scandalous at the time, she could never talk about it. I bet the child is hidden in the house somewhere. Wilma's grandfather told her that the old mansion has a false wall on the second floor." Peaches's eyes were bright as she considered this mysterious possibility.

"I don't think so, Peaches," I said, thinking of places where Millie could hide someone. The guest rooms were usually full, and even the haunted Tower Suite was booked this weekend. Millie kept three rooms to herself at the back of the house, facing her garden, but I had been in those rooms, too, and there wasn't anybody else living there. And I hadn't noticed any doors leading to nowhere, or walls that looked like they didn't belong.

"Well, it makes for a good story, anyway." She sat back and patted her tummy. Belched and smiled like a contented cat. "Speaking of stories, how is your story coming?"

"I've got almost two hundred pages," I said proudly.

Peaches smiled.

"You gonna let me read them?"

I shook my head.

"Journey's not over yet."

"OK. So what's next on your to-do list? You've conquered a small town, turned around a restaurant business, gained some entrepreneurial skills, and absorbed some local folklore. I assume you are now well versed in indigenous American affairs, too." She looked at Jess when she said this and cleared her throat.

I shook my head as I lit a cigarette.

"Don't go there."

Peaches shrugged, reached for one of my Kools. "OK. So where are *you* going next? I assume that you aren't going to stay here forever."

To tell the truth, I hadn't thought about it. I was happy and content right here in Paper Moon, even though it was totally different from everything I had ever known and I was working harder than I'd ever worked. I had found myself a place, a job, even some friends. But Peaches was right. I was on a journey. I was a heroine creating an adventure. Adventures didn't stand still. And romantic heroines didn't work in diners out in the middle of nowhere. Did they?

Or *did* they?

"I'm heading for California in a few weeks. I've got a new account and I'll be hauling electronics. Oakland, Los Angeles, San Diego. And back again in October. Have you got the urge to see Hollywood?"

"Yeah, I do," I told her.

But I wasn't sure.

I wanted to see the ocean, and maybe even go down into Mexico. With the money I was earning at the diner, I could actually do that. I had been reading a book about

Hawaii. I thought, maybe I'd work for a few months in Los Angeles, scrape together the money to go to Hawaii. After that, who knew?

But something inside me kept saying, "Wait." It said, "Look at the mountains a little longer. Walk along the lake and listen to the birds. Watch the deer, and hear the wind whistle in the pines." Something was holding me back. As if part of my adventure was still here, hidden, in little Paper Moon.

"When you goin'?" I asked Peaches, in an effort to clear my head.

"End of September, early October. I'll call you. I should be back through here the week of the twenty-ninth. That oughta give you enough time to get your fill of small-town Montana life."

I told her I would think about it.

Jess was still on the phone when Peaches left. Not that I really cared—those one-handed pancakes had turned out all right.

It was just strange, though. Jess's phone conversations usually lasted one minute or less, and consisted of a few grunts, a "Yeah" or a "No," and then he would hang up. He never talked to anyone (that I knew of) besides his family: Mary, her husband, Raymond, or the kids. Or me. Unless he was ordering for the diner, of course. And those conversations lasted two minutes instead of one.

I came back to the counter and he turned toward the grill, his voice low.

I started chopping up hard-boiled eggs for my tuna salad. Fish Reynolds and the boys just loved my tuna salad on wheat toast.

"Yeah . . . OK . . . well, just keep your nose clean. I'll

send you the money . . . I know . . . I got it. . . ." Jess jotted something down on the pad next to the refrigerator. "OK, I'll take care of it . . . no . . . I won't . . ."

"Juanita, you making chicken salad, too?" Mignon leaned over the counter watching me as I chopped up the eggs, celery, and onion.

"Nope, it's Juanita-feel-like day," I told her, wiping my eye with the back of my hand. I needed to get some Vidalia onions. They never made me cry.

Mignon's pretty face twisted into a frown, then she giggled.

"I think I know the answer to this, but I'm going to ask anyway. What is Juanita-feel-like day?"

I grinned at her.

"It means that we're having whatever Juanita feels like for lunch. And Juanita feels like tuna salad."

"You and Peaches are friends?" Jess asked me after she left.

I watched her climb up into the big, purple cab of the Kenworth, and wave.

"She was the one who brought me here. Recommended your place for breakfast as a matter of fact." I looked at him sideways.

"She tells me she's going to California and that you're going with her."

I shrugged my shoulders, stamped out the eighth cigarette I'd smoked in an hour and reached for my apron. I really needed to quit smoking.

"I might. I might not."

Jess's eyes flickered for a moment.

"You know that you can stay here as long as you want."

"I know."

"Mignon says I oughta make you a partner."

I smiled, thinking of Mignon's efforts to match up her uncle and me. On the surface we were like oil and water— Jess was silent, I was talkative. I was stubborn and moving on; Jess was easygoing and staying put. We didn't seem to have much in common. But looks were deceiving. Mignon said I didn't really know Jess. I told her I didn't have half a century to do that. But to tell you the truth, I knew almost as much as I needed to know. Jess's quiet eyes told quite a story.

"Mignon just likes my barbecued ribs, that's all."

Jess grunted. That was his way of laughing.

"Well, think about it."

I threw two steaks on the grill.

"Think about what?"

"About what I said."

With that, I snapped. I turned on Jess, hands on hips, my head bobbing.

"Jess Gardiner, I am sick and tired of these damn three-word-sentence conversations we always seem to have. You want to ask me this, and ask me that. But you ain't asked me shit! You don't say 'Juanita, let's sit down and talk about so and so.' You don't say 'I'd like for you to think about this, or think about that.' You just grunt and glare, and spit out four words, and leave. Really pisses me off."

The yuppie couple from Denver turned red, and pretended to be studying their menus. Carl was grinning as he bussed the dishes.

Jess didn't say anything.

And I couldn't tell you why I was jumping on him that way. He had given me a job. And the job had given me a sense of my own value. I was doing something I was really good at. And I was appreciated for it. In many ways, he had given me my place. And here I was, yelling at him like he'd stolen something. It must have been seeing Peaches again. Made me think too much. About things I hadn't done.

The ringing of the telephone kept me from saying something else stupid that I would regret.

Jess answered the phone. I stabbed at the steaks searing on the grill. Mad at Peaches for making me remember that it was probably time to move on. Mad at Jess for making me want to stay here. Mad at myself for not being able to make up my mind. I was lost in my thoughts and the smoke coming up from the grill when I heard Jess's voice.

"Yes, she's here, but she's busy. Yes. I'll give her the message, but no, she ain't gonna call you back, Rashawn. Naw, brother man, I'm her boss and her friend. What's that? Yeah, well, you do what you gotta do. Your mother's busy, and she doesn't have time for this. Looks like you might have to solve that problem yourself, huh. Later."

"That was Rashawn?" I felt my jaws getting tight.

He was the last person I'd want to hear from. So, he'd be the first to call. It made me mad. Some weeks ago, in a moment of weakness, I gave Bertie the number at the diner "for emergencies only." Needless to say, Rashawn's definition of "emergency" and mine don't match.

Jess hung up the phone and shrugged.

"Yep. And before you do a neutron dance on my head, woman, he was calling collect to get five hundred dollars from you for bail money. I don't suppose that's how you want to spend your hard-earned cash."

"It ain't none of your damn business how I want to spend my money," I snapped back at him, angry because he had meddled in my business, angrier because that fool son of mine was finally in jail, and had the nerve to track me down and squeeze me for cash again. Just like old times.

"Maybe, maybe not. But I do know that you don't need this aggravation. He's grown, Juanita. He can take care of himself."

"Look, you just stay out of my life, OK? I'll take my own telephone calls from now on, you don't have to run interference for me. I can handle these things. I don't need you, of all people, to tell me how to run my life!"

I saw Jess's jaw tighten, and he glared at me for a second then shook his head.

"Juanita, what you need is . . ."

The screen door opened and a dozen campers came through, talking and laughing loudly. I went to the refrigerator and pulled out two cartons of eggs. Jess got them seated. As he passed me on his way to the back, he stopped at the counter, and said very softly, "Look, Juanita, whatever you want to do is fine with me as long as it makes *you* happy. I don't really care. I just don't want to lose you."

The funny feeling I'd gotten in my stomach the first time I met him had come back. And it wasn't hunger.

Suddenly I realized how much *I* really had to lose.

Chapter Fourteen

I found Millie on the porch one evening when I got back from shopping in Missoula. It was mean of me, I know, but I sneaked up on her when I saw she was sitting in the porch swing with that mysterious Siamese cat. This was the first time I'd actually seen her holding that cat, although I'd seen her talk to it many times, especially at night. Come to think of it, you hardly ever saw that cat in the day.

I came 'round the back way, stood behind the rose-bushes. Held my breath because roses make me sneeze. Listened to the wind kicking up in the pine trees. Listened to Millie croon to that cat in a funny-sounding language.

Didn't hide long, though. Those roses got the best of me, and I sneezed and coughed at the same time. Millie laughed at me.

"Goodness, Juanita, why are you hiding in the bushes? You'd think you'd stole something! Come, sit down with me and Asim. It's a lovely night even though Antonio says it's going to rain soon." She looked up and squinted. "I can still see the stars."

"Asim?" I said, sniffling and sneezing as I came out of the bush and walked up the steps.

Millie smiled and stroked the purring cat, who was now lying in her lap.

"Asim. You've seen him before, of course."

I patted the Siamese, who studied me carefully with icy-blue eyes.

"Of course," I repeated. I sat down in the rocking chair and pulled out a tissue. "Just set me straight, though. Is he an ex-husband, too?"

Millie smiled and stared off into space. Asim looked at me as if I had stolen something. She did not answer my question.

"I'm taking a creative writing course at UM Extension," Millie said, not answering the question. "We've been doing character studies, poetry, essays for weeks. Now the instructor has assigned our first real, nitty-gritty writing project. A short story, a few thousand words. To be developed later into a novella. How exciting!"

Asim blinked at me. I blinked back.

"What are you going to write about?"

Millie adjusted Asim on her lap.

"Well, it's a good thing you sneaked by when you did. I've been turning this idea around in my head for a couple of days now, and I think it's time I tried it out on a real, live person. I asked Inez to be my guinea pig, but she says she only likes mysteries. And Elma Van Roan is partial to tragedies." Asim purred loudly. Millie lifted him up and gave him a kiss. "And this is a romance.

"It's 1935, Kenya, a little north of Nairobi. Oh, Juanita, it's such beautiful country with clear, ethereal lakes; majestic, mysterious mountains with snowcapped peaks. Like Montana, but not like Montana. There's a huge British population there with the usual, boring regulars, their wives and underlings. And the native people, who begrudgingly tolerate them, even as they plot to overthrow them.

"There's an American entertainer visiting a friend for a few months. She's recovering from her last love affair. She entertains at a party, given by the commanding officer of the regiment stationed in Nairobi. And she falls in love with a wealthy coffee planter."

Asim's purring got louder. I wondered if he was all right. Looked up to find him looking up at Millie. She was still talking, a wistful smile on her face, her eyes unseeing and distant.

"They began a passionate affair. It really was scandalous! You see, he was married, but his wife lived in Pretoria." She giggled. "The singer moved into the planter's huge plantation, had her own suite of rooms, servants, elephants, everything! It was like living in a dream." Millie sighed.

"Of course, everyone was against this liaison. The British socialites were humiliated, but didn't know what to do. The singer was wild, and gay, totally uninhibited. Very different from the prim and proper English matrons who made up the white population there.

"Their affair went on for over a year, but then things in Kenya got bad. Really bad. The Mau Mau were everywhere, and the white people were afraid. The planter had reconciled himself to black rule, and even worked with the revolutionaries to plan a peaceful change of power. But the times were dangerous . . . and soon it became very clear that the planter was committed to his land, and its people, and the singer . . . well . . . life in the outback of Kenya was tolerable for a short period of time, but she soon yearned for the bright lights of New York and Paris and London. And besides, there were war clouds forming over Germany . . ." Millie paused for a moment.

"They were so different yet their hearts were so much alike. But they knew it wasn't possible for them to remain in paradise forever. He had a duty to his new country. She . . ." Millie's voice broke, and I looked up, surprised to find tears streaming down her face. She continued speaking in a whisper. "She knew that, while it was easy to stay in paradise, it was better, even braver perhaps, to leave. She still had mountains of her own to climb. Even though she left everything she ever loved in his hands."

Asim meowed loudly. Stood up and rubbed against her. Millie shushed him, and wiped the tears from her face. Spoke to him again in words I did not recognize.

"Did you leave him?" I asked, knowing that she had.

Millie nodded, unable to speak.

"What happened to the coffee planter?"

"He served the new Kenya long and well," she whispered, dropping tears on Asim, who didn't seem to mind.

"Is he still alive?"

Millie looked up at me, her eyes wet, her face drawn and unhappy.

"It's a story, Juanita, remember?"

I lit a cigarette.

"And the singer? What happened to her? In your story, I mean."

Millie laughed.

"Why, she owns a bed-and-breakfast in Paper Moon, Montana, of course."

"Of course," I repeated.

Asim meowed again, rubbed against Millie, then jumped down from the swing and disappeared around the side of the house.

Millie looked up at the sky. When she spoke again, her voice was strange and distant, haunted in a way, like Elma Van Roan.

"The professor wants us to block out the first draft in the form of a parable, like Aesop's fables. With a moral at the end."

"And the moral of your story?"

"Well, I'm still working on that," Millie said slowly. "But if I had to guess, I'd say that sometimes, when you love someone, you have to let go, even if it's not what you want to do. And the other person has to have the courage to leave, if it's necessary, to finish the goals they set for themselves. Lovers have to allow themselves the freedom to do what they must. That's the greatest love there is. Otherwise . . ." she paused, stared off into space again. "Otherwise, it becomes a prison. And the love will wither away and die like most things do when they're locked away like that."

"Did she ever see him again?"

Millie didn't answer me. Just got up off that swing, and went inside. And just before the screen door hit the doorjamb, the Siamese slipped in behind her.

I stayed there for a moment. Thought about the story she'd told me. Was it something she made up? Or was it really a part of her life a long, long time ago? I thought about her love affair with a man she could never have and had to leave behind. Wondered if Paris and London and New York were ever worth what he had given her. Thought about love, and possession and . . . freedom.

In my life, I had never known love without possession. I had always been So-and-so's wife, I had always gone where they had gone, I had done what they had wanted. I thought that I was loved and had loved in return by doing those things. It had not occurred to me that love could go with freedom.

Peaches was coming back in a few weeks and I could hitch a ride with her to California, and maybe on from there to Mexico.

I looked up at the Pleiades. Saw Jess's face there.

Wondered if it was time for me to leave. Or time for me to stay.

Chapter Fifteen

I love the sound of a summer storm.

It had started right around seven on Saturday, just as I was closing up. We closed early that weekend because the county fair was on. I was in a funny mood, had been all day, so I sent Carl home early. Wished Jess would leave, too, but he was knocking around in the back. I didn't know what he was doing, and didn't care really. Just as long as he left me alone. I wanted the place to myself.

The dishes were washed and dried, the tables wiped clean. The salt and pepper shakers were filled, catsup and mustard put away. I seasoned the granddaddy skillet, left it on the back burner, sliced the butter for breakfast, and set it in the refrigerator.

The front door was open and I looked out. Watched that storm roll in from Idaho, saw the sky grow black, zigzags of silver snapping toward the ground. The pines swayed. The wind was picking up.

I sniffed the air, and I could smell the rain before I saw it. The air was heavy with it. The thunder rumbled in the background. The lights went off for a few seconds, the old generator groaned. Then the lights came back on, a little reluctantly it seemed to me. The rain came down with a vengeance. I smiled to myself, closed my eyes, and listened to the rain hitting the roof. The stiff, sticky late-August heat was gone for the moment, the temperature had dropped almost fifteen degrees. Good sleeping weather. I thought about the raindrops dancing on Arcadia Lake.

A crack of thunder woke Dracula, who whined a little, then yawned. He licked his paws and rolled over.

Jess carried in a box of steaks, set them in the freezer. He yelled at me as he went out the back door.

"You want a ride to Millie's?"

"Nope."

"You sure?"

"I'm sure."

He clicked his tongue at Dracula, who looked up, then put his head under his paws. Jess frowned. Whistled this time. Poor Dracula sighed and dragged himself up and followed Jess out.

Jess yelled, "Better move it. It's gonna rain."

I looked outside. It was pouring.

"No shit," I said to no one in particular. I glanced over my shoulder. Jess was gone.

I checked out the window, saw man and dog scramble into the old pickup, then turn onto the road and disappear into the thick forest nearby. Kaylin's Ridge and Jess's cabin weren't too far away.

I turned out the lights, checked the pilot light on the

stove, and locked up. Opened my umbrella. I walked out of there with every intention of making a break for it to Millie's, taking a long, hot bath, and collapsing into bed.

But the storm stopped me. I just stood on the porch, with my little fold-up umbrella over my head, watching the storm, listening to the raindrops dance on the tin roof of Henry's Citgo across the way. For a half hour or more, I watched. And listened. Listening to the water speed through the rain pipes, splashing on the concrete slab on the side of the diner, like a waterfall gone mad. I watched a wall of water move over the town and drench it, then move on into the mountains above. The clouds, now released of their burden, lightened in color from steel gray to fine silver blue, and the sun tried here and there to peek through, but the clouds were still too thick with the moisture left behind. The lightning sliced through the air in the distance now, and I figured that Missoula was in for a big rain.

Paper Moon was now left with a fine, light downpour, the kind you can see through, the kind that helps you sleep, or inspires the poet to write. Heavy enough to get you wet, but light enough for a robin to fly through if she wants.

I took a deep breath, and caught the scent of the forest in the moist air. Just a hint of pine, a rich aroma of the warm earth and the thick, sweet smell of flowers.

I listened for the thunder again. Looked for lightning.

And when I didn't hear it, and didn't see it, I dropped my tote bag on the porch, closed my umbrella, slipped off my sandals, and walked down the slope toward the lake.

I have always wanted to dance in the rain. People do it in the movies all the time. Couples stroll together hand in hand in the rain. But no one ever seems to do it for real. There are always umbrellas up, stained khaki-colored raincoats, floppy shapeless hats and rubber boots. No one wants to get wet. They want to keep dry, to be protected. Being wet never hurt anybody, did it?

The grass squished under my feet, and I got smacked in the face by a tree branch that I didn't see. By the time I reached the lakeshore, I was soaked to the skin.

There was a little clearing there, just a small patch of grass, and then the rocks leading to the water. It wasn't big enough for a lakeside barbecue, but it was big enough for me.

I stopped there and listened to the rhythm of the rain as it hit the water and the trees nearby. I pulled the sounds and the beat into my head. I absorbed it, I breathed it.

And then I danced.

I lifted my arms to the rain goddess and danced a ring-around-the-rosy. The water dribbled down my arms and I licked it off my fingers, slurped it from the palms of my hands.

I pirouetted on my toes—a stiff ballerina—and closed my eyes as I lifted my arms up and down, up and down. Swan Lake . . . I imagined myself on a stage in old St. Petersburg, the star of the ballet company, dancing for the czar, dancing from my heart.

I made a tribute to the Motherland—patting my feet to a rhythm as old as the rain itself, maybe older. Clapping my wet hands together, rubbing the wetness across my breasts and down my abdomen. Shaking my behind as I moved around, the rain provided the drums and the chant.

There was something ancient here and I was a part of it. The forest around the lake was lush green and dripping with moisture. The rain, cool and steady, danced on the lake and with the ninety-degree heat, I could see steam rising in places, or was it fog? The mists gave my little clearing a mystical quality, the spirits of the lake were here, and I was one of them, dancing, praying, paying tribute to the earth, drinking her wine, caressing her body with my thumping feet. I inhaled the rich honeysuckle incense she was burning, thick and sweet, in the damp air.

Behind me, a twig snapped. The magical mist lifted for a moment. I stopped moving. I wasn't really worried that someone would think I was crazy—I didn't care a rat's ass about that.

But I was by myself. And Arcadia Lake was back off the highway, isolated and out of sight. Paper Moon, Montana, was a popular truck stop, it was right off the interstate. As Peaches would say, you never knew what kind of serial killers might be driving those big rigs.

I froze and looked around me, but there was no one there. Still, I had heard something. Snap. There it was again. It came from the left. Near the honeysuckle bush. I felt a pair of eyes studying me. I glanced around quickly. Nothing there. But I still felt someone, or something, watching me. Then I looked down. I had almost missed him.

Tiny, beady black eyes, a dark stripe down his back and he was as still as a rock—holding his breath and hoping I wouldn't see him.

A chipmunk. Watching me intently, waiting for me to turn away so he could make his move.

Well, I didn't move. But I did sneeze. And little Alvin, he squeaked, jumped at least six inches, and scurried away, twigs and leaves crackling under his tiny feet.

I laughed. Not a giggle. Not a chuckle. A belly laugh. I

laughed until my sides ached. What the hell was I doing, anyway? Poor little thing, he probably thought I was the craziest human he'd ever seen! Here I was, somebody's grandmother, living hundreds of miles away from home among strangers, a runaway, fearless (well, sort of), and soaked to the skin and dancing barefoot in the rain like a pagan worshiper carried away by the spirit. And spooked by a tiny chipmunk.

I had to be crazy. It was wonderful.

And I laughed again. Laughed until my eyes watered. Laughed until I coughed and my stomach hurt.

"You left your tote bag . . ."

I whirled around to find Jess behind me, my tote bag hanging from his outstretched hand. How long had he been standing there? I didn't know whether to be angry or awed. I had heard a four-ounce chipmunk, and this one-hundred-eighty-pound man hadn't made one sound.

Damn Lakota . . .

"Just set it there, I don't need it," I snapped, aggravated that he had seen me. Angry that he had intruded on my ceremony, and interrupted my private dance.

"You were dancing," he said flatly.

"That's what I like about you, Jess," I grumbled. "You always state the obvious."

There I was, snapping at him again.

"In the rain . . ."

"Do you want to join me?" I challenged him.

His black eyes flickered for a moment but he never took them from my face. And I saw . . .

"You were laughing."

"Well, Jess, it's not a crime," I retorted, annoyed with

him. I reached for my tote bag and he moved it out of my reach.

"I've never heard you laugh like that before."

"I do it once a year on the fourth Saturday of August whether I need to or not. You ought to try it sometime, Lakota Man. That's what's wrong with you. You have no sense of humor and no passion. Now, give me . . ." Even when I said it, I knew that it wasn't true.

I tried to snatch my dripping bag from him again, but he pulled it away, and me toward him.

His usually quiet eyes were stormy and fierce, hot with intensity, and with another quality that I could not describe. The fact that they were black in color did not detract from the sparks I felt down to my toes. My stomach tied into an uncomfortable knot—and I suddenly realized how the little chipmunk must have felt. I wanted to stay and I wanted to run.

"Don't tell me I have no passion," he said evenly before he kissed me.

What happened after that only comes to me now like a dream that I had, and now that I am awake, only the golds and the blues, the silvers and the whites come through in my mind. It is all sensory: how I felt, how he felt, what I smelled and tasted, no linear scenes, no sense of time or space, as if our loving was not real, but a dream and relegated to the subconscious realms of my mind. The coolness of early evening, the smell of wet skin and honeysuckle, always the honeysuckle, thick and sweet, its scent rich and warm, these are the things that are the clearest.

I don't know how we got to his cabin. I don't even remember walking up the slopes to the road. The very next memory that comes to mind is his face as he lay me gently onto the pillows of his bed, and the sweet words he whispered in my ear in an ancient language I could not understand.

He undressed me slowly and almost reverently, the wet clothes peeled away from my skin like thin layers of silk until I lay naked, and wet and burning from a fire within.

He worshiped me first with his eyes, then with his hands. Then, his lips.

I would have blushed had I known how, but I was beyond that. It must have been the reverence in his eyes that made me hold his gaze, that eased my fears, that caused my nipples to harden and my thighs to weaken. He studied me carefully, without words, without expression, but with a fire in his eyes that kept me warm despite the cool evening breeze that floated through the open window.

I awoke from my dreamlike state only once when I remembered the imperfect condition of my body, and became self-conscious and ashamed. I moved to cover myself with my hands, but he stopped me, taking my hands from my breasts, his eyes never leaving mine.

He kissed the knees that I felt were lumpy and fat, and ran his tongue up my thighs until they quivered and parted. He traced the tiny, silver slivers which crisscrossed my belly and stroked the loosened skin with his hands, telling me that I must have been exquisite when I was pregnant so long ago. By the time his tongue reached my nipples, I was delirious, my body running hot and cold. He licked the beads of sweat from my forehead, and wrapped his strong body around mine to keep me from shivering. I moaned for him to release me but he shushed me with his kisses.

He touched me with such gentleness that I wondered at first if he thought I might break, or that I might be offended somehow. But I soon learned that his gentleness was just his way of paying homage to me. I felt as if I was worth twice my weight in gold and diamonds.

And when he moved inside me, I couldn't think at all. The words to describe what I was feeling deserted me, and I became instinctive, primal, and wordless, letting my body speak for me, telling him with every kiss, every touch, every moan, and every squeeze, what it was I really wanted—and how I really felt about him.

And I had said he had no passion.

I now knew why we had often said so few words to each other. I had known from the day I met him. For weeks, I had been reading his thoughts in his eyes.

Later, while Jess was sleeping, I stepped out onto the porch and listened to the sounds of a night recovering from the brilliant noises of a summer storm. I didn't hear any scurrying or rustling in the undergrowth. The critters had more sense than I had. They had burrowed into their dens and nests and settled themselves to sleep.

The thunderstorm was long gone, and all we were left with was a light, misty spray. But in the distance, the thunder rumbled now and then as if to remind us that it could still come back and threaten us with its booming voice.

And I listened to my heartbeat and remembered the warm touch of Jess's fingertips on my damp skin. And smiled to myself.

Chapter Sixteen

I divided my time between Jess's cabin and Millie's place. Sometimes it was just better to go to Millie's and chitchat, stroke the cats, and eat Irene's fudge. Other times, when I needed to hear his voice, speaking only to me, and feel his hand gently stroke my face and my hair, I made my way up the mountain to Jess's cabin.

Millie said I had a split personality.

But Jess didn't seem to mind. And I began to think that with us working together all day, too, it might be pushing it to wrap ourselves up in each other twenty-four-seven. We were too old for that puppy love stuff. That's what I told myself.

"You're treating me like a whore," Jess told me one night after we had both melted into a muddle of sighs. He was still wrapped around me, his legs holding mine in a tight embrace, his thighs tightening their muscles and then releasing. He had propped himself up on his elbow and, even in the dark, I could feel his eyes boring into mine. But there was only warmth there. And amusement. I touched his face and felt that the corners of his mouth were turned upward into a grin.

"What are you talking about?" I wrinkled my nose and blew a raspberry at him. His hair had fallen down into my face. I pulled a strand and he yelped. He licked my nose.

"You treat me like a whore," he repeated, tracing the outlines of several O's on my breast. I closed my eyes. "You only use me for sex . . ." He licked my nipple and I gasped. "And you don't pay me!"

I swatted at him and giggled.

"I'm using you on credit," I gasped. "Anyway, I think you should pay *me*," I told him, gasping again as his hand found a certain spot that I hadn't known I had. "Besides, this is sexual harassment. You are my boss, you know."

I could feel his chest rise and fall as he chuckled.

"Hell, Juanita. I ain't been the boss of that diner since you set foot in the place three months ago!"

We giggled together in the dark. Two middle-aged love buddies working on a second chance. Second chance? It was probably the last chance for both of us. Our laughter melted into sighs again and then silence. I hugged Jess tighter than I had ever held any man in my life. He was real enough. But in case I was dreaming, I wanted to grab on to the dream for as long as I could.

"When are you going to California?" Jess asked later. He slipped a heavy robe over my shoulders and sat down behind me, cradling me within his arms.

"I don't know when I'm going."

Jess frowned, leaning forward to look at me. I avoided his eyes.

"I don't know if I'm going."

He growled at me.

"What do you mean, you don't know 'if' you're going? What the hell . . ."

"Maybe . . ." I saw the Pacific in my mind's eye: deep-green and vast. The reds, oranges, and browns of Mexico danced in my imagination. I thought about adventures to come, but now, they seemed a million miles, a million years away. Jess's face kept intruding on my daydreams.

There was a place in my heart for him. A place that was only his.

But was there a place in my great adventures for him? Even the ones that were only pipe dreams?

"Maybe . . . I'll just stay here . . ."

"You'll just stay here? Juanita, that don't make any sense now. You've been talking about California and Mexico and Vancouver . . . forever . . ." He stopped. He hadn't known me forever but it sure seemed like it. "Ever since I've known you. Why wouldn't you go? Why would you pass it up?"

He looked at me for a long time.

I looked away.

I had an answer on the tip of my tongue, but it sounded ignorant. Because I have a man now? I couldn't even believe that I was thinking that way! And I was not going to say that aloud. It sounded like some fourteen-year-old. I shrugged my shoulders as if I was trying to shake off an unwelcome hand. I heard Jess take a deep breath.

"I . . . uh . . ." I struggled to come up with an answer.

Jess shook me by the shoulders. Shook me hard.

"Listen to me, woman. If it's me you're thinking about?

If this has something to do with us?" He paused again. I knew that he was measuring his words, choosing them carefully, arranging and rearranging them in his head.

His voice, when he finally spoke again, was low and hoarse.

"Juanita, I want you to listen, OK? Don't interrupt me. I love you. You make me smile. You make me laugh. You piss me off more than anybody I've ever met. You've shone a light into a place in my heart where I thought no light would ever shine."

He stopped for a moment. I was crying. He kissed the tip of my nose. His lips were gentle and soft. But his eyes were still fierce.

"But if you think for a minute that I would let you just stay here, you're crazier than I always knew you were! I don't want you to 'just stay here.' Listen, African Queen, if you love me enough to give up your great adventure, well, I love you enough to give up the urge to chain you to my bed and let you go to California, or Timbuktu, or wherever the hell else you want to go." He stopped again. "Do you understand what I'm saying to you?"

I didn't really. Because no one had ever said that to me before.

"But . . . don't you want me to stay here? With you?"

I thought about Jess, about his feelings. About the losses that already haunted him. I didn't want to add to that.

"Yes. But what do *you* want?"

I didn't know how to answer that question.

I couldn't remember anyone ever asking me what I wanted. No man ever did anyway.

"I wouldn't have to go alone. You could come with me."

Jess shook his head and chuckled. His hair caressed my shoulders. He kissed me on the back of my neck.

"Did it. Took the hero's tour of Da Nang and Saigon, survived in one piece. Bummed around Europe afterward. Went to New York and did stir-fry, baked quiche in L.A. It's your turn, Juanita. And you've got to do it alone."

"How do you know I'll come back?" I challenged him.

What a stupid question.

Jess's eyes softened.

"I don't know here," he answered, tapping his head lightly with his finger. "But I *do* know here." He took my hands in his and put them to his heart.

"This. *This* is Juanita's place. Always."

I leaned against him and closed my eyes. Listened to the wind blowing through the trees. The sounds were whispery and soft. And I was glad to be home at last.

I pretty much stopped staying at Millie's after that.

I walked to work one day a week later. Jess was opening up.

The night before, I had worked the dinner shift and we'd had a huge crowd. It was nonstop. I couldn't remember seeing so many folks on a Wednesday night. My feet hurt and my back felt like the Denver Broncos had done a tap dance on it. Jess had rubbed my feet and put the heating pad on my back and brought me tea. I thought I was the Queen of Sheba.

I felt better in the morning, told Jess I wanted a cheese omelet with parsley and sausage links. He said he'd fix me a bowl of Cheerios and left, slamming the door. I smiled. I knew that I would probably have my omelet, parsley, sausage, coffee, and a rose in a bud vase waiting on me by the time I got to the diner.

I had a lot more than that.

As I strolled down the mountain and reached the highway, a curious scene caught my eye. It was a study in contrasts. And I was so amazed by the differences and the drama that the meaning of what I saw didn't hit me until later.

In the pure, morning sun, the diner looked like a relic from the wild west, rustic and rough, its dark wood a stark contrast to the soft orange-blue sky and the deep, velvety green of the tall Montana pines. The parking lot, slate in color and still coarse gravel in places, added to the feeling of the scene, and, rising off in the distance, the mountains stood, looming over it all, snowcapped here and there. The sun was relentless, brilliant, and orange like the imported tangerines I had been buying for their tangy juice. The morning air was getting cooler now—it was moving into October—and the crispness had a color, too, sharp and pungent, even though it didn't have a smell. Teal. That's what it was. It hit my nose like ice. Teal. It felt like teal would if it had been a sensation or a thing rather than a color.

And in the middle of it, right smack in the midst of the slate gray of the parking lot, staring up at the mountain and silhouetted by the strangely colored morning sky and the old, ghost town–looking building that was the diner, stood a man. A black man dressed in jeans and a baggy shirt and dreadlocks twisting around his head like tiny, hairy snakes.

He looked almost as out of place here as I did.

It made a pretty picture: the urban man and the wild, rural mountainside. I sketched it out.

Mignon had talked me into taking art lessons at the community college's extension campus. I had been going twice a week for the past month and I loved it. Thought I was Renoir or somebody. But my "style," if you could call it anything, was more like Grandma Moses.

I started to draw the scene in my mind: the craggy sides of the mountains in the background; the texture of the huge evergreens up close; a stroke here and a stroke there for the millions of needles and the old, worn-down and ancient-looking diner, its sides rough and wind-burned.

"Texture! Add texture!" I could hear my teacher coaxing me.

I added the granules of gravel, circular and square and triangular, bits here and there, like the Impressionists I had been studying, dots and dots and dots of gray. I added the rusted sides of the old GMC truck cab that Roger Schumacher drove.

Then I added the colors of Montana—the brilliant orangy-red gold of the sun; the deep sapphire of the sky and the evergreen—was there another word that would do as well?—the evergreen of the forest, winding up the mountainside toward a little dark brown cabin where, at times, you could see the silver ribbon of smoke curling upward from an invisible chimney.

Against this backdrop, I added the nut brown–colored man, dressed in his faded jeans, a brown and tan baggy shirt, and the huge, black Frankenstein shoes he wore that probably weighed a ton. His back was turned so I couldn't see his face, but I drew it in my mind. He was looking up toward Kaylin's Ridge.

I knew that this city boy—and that's what he had to be (how many dreadlocked, baggy-shirted, brougham shoe–wearing colored boys lived in Montana?)—had never seen anything like this little ridge here, wedged in between a small mountain range and a huge, jewel-colored lake, except in movies. I figured that he had spent his life riding buses or the subway, and that he might live in a high-rise apartment building. It amused me and made me sad at the same time to think that this boy had probably never ridden a horse. I was sure that he had never watched deer tiptoe delicately to the water's edge and sip in the early-morning hours. The only thing this boy had done in the early-morning hours was tiptoe into his apartment, his shoes in his hands, trying not to wake his parents at five A.M.

This boy was used to seeing tall, modern buildings, and listening to car horns while he dodged city buses. He was used to walking fast at night, and hoping that the police didn't stop him and ask what he was doing. He might go to the park sometimes in the summer and hang out with his boys and smoke cigarettes and drink beer, but he had never trudged up a mountain ridge, strolled along a lake-shore, or stared out across a plain.

He stood completely still. Wasn't moving at all, just looking. He was standing almost in the same spot I had stood months ago when Peaches dropped me off in the diner's parking lot. I remember looking up at the ridge and down at Lake Arcadia and wondering what kind of world I had lived in all my life.

Then it dawned on me.

That it wasn't just a man standing there.

It was Randy.

My son.

He heard my feet hit the crunchy gravel and turned around. In his too-mature face I saw wonder at the beautiful Montana landscape but not much surprise at seeing me.

"Hello, Momma."

"Randy?" It was the only thing that I could think of to say.

He grinned, his dark face crinkling in places that even I didn't have wrinkles as yet. There were circles under his eyes. That made me sad. Life in the penitentiary hadn't been easy. But it was still a nice face. And in his tired but sparkling dark brown eyes I could still see the laughing face of my first baby.

I started crying.

He folded me into his arms. I hugged him tight.

"Don't cry, Momma. It's OK. It's all right now."

I pushed back from him but still held on to his arms. They were firm and muscled. Not like the old Randy.

I looked my boy in the face.

"You haven't . . . you didn't . . ." I couldn't bring myself to form the words.

He laughed at me, his white teeth still clean and even. He shook his head, still smiling. He kissed me on the cheek.

"No, Momma," Randy said firmly. He was amused at my attempts to question him. "No, I didn't break out. No, I didn't run away. Or kill a guard or scale the wall."

Of course my expression was asking him the next question.

Randy shrugged his shoulders.

"They let me out. A shock probation program that the state just put in. I've kept myself together, didn't bother nobody, and minded my own business. Been taking ac-counting courses. Tutored some of the younger guys in math . . ."

I wiped the tears away from my cheeks. Tried to focus on my boy's face through my bleary eyes.

"You were always good at math," I murmured.

"Yes, ma'am," he agreed. "And something else, too, Momma . . ."

Yes, ma'am? The last time that boy called me "ma'am" he was ten years old. Things *had* changed.

"What else, Randy?" I reached for the canvas backpack that he was carrying.

"I've been teaching Sunday school, Momma," Randy said quickly as if he was out of breath rushing to get the words out in one blow.

Sunday school? I stared at him.

In the back of my mind was the image of three little kids dressed in navy blue and white (Bertie wore the white). They were squirming because their Sunday shoes were a little stiff and they were anxious to go play outside rather than sit through a lesson on Jonah and the whale.

His voice was low and serious. His dark eyes held mine with a pleading look. As if he wanted me to give him something. As if he wanted my approval.

"I found Jesus, Momma," he finally spit it out. Then he looked at me again with the hopeful, wishing look.

I stroked his cheek and pulled the backpack off his shoulder.

"Jesus wasn't never lost, Randy," I told him. "You were the one that was lost." I nudged him toward the diner. "And now . . . you're found."

Randy chuckled then and took the backpack away from me.

"All right, Momma."

Jess's eyes never blinked when I walked in the door with Randy behind me. He looked over his shoulder at us, flipped a pancake, and went back to turning the sausage.

I should have known then.

He started fussing.

"Juanita! I've been trying to keep your omelet warm here while you spend your time socializing, but you know eggs don't keep too well. It'll be your own fault if they taste like Play-Doh."

I showed Randy a table and went to get him a plate and some coffee.

"Jess, this is my son, Randy. Randy, this is Jess Gardiner."

Jess didn't even turn around.

"Your trip all right, Randy?" Jess asked, his words clipped and sharp.

"Yes, sir," my prodigal son replied. He nodded at Mignon who dropped off a glass of orange juice. I thought she winked at him but maybe I was seeing things.

"You have enough money for food and everything along the way?"

"Yes, sir," came the next reply right on cue.

"Well, if you've got money left over, I should be getting some change, shouldn't I?"

Randy grinned.

I was confused.

Change?

"What change?" I asked, grabbing a blueberry muffin from the tray that Carl had just brought out. Randy loved blueberry muffins.

Jess slapped three Montana-sized pancakes on a platter and snatched up a quartet of sausage links as a garnish. I put the muffin back. Randy had always been my skinny child. No way he was going to eat three state-sized pancakes, sausage, eggs, and a blueberry muffin—in one sitting.

"I gave him one hundred and fifty dollars," came the terse reply. "Randy, the bus ticket was only sixty bucks. I know you didn't eat up ninety dollars worth of food in a day and a half! I took the gray dog across the U.S. back in seventy-seven. Never knew anyone who could eat ninety dollars worth of McDonald's in that short a time."

A hundred and fifty dollars? I stared at my son and at Jess. But I wasn't even in this conversation.

They both ignored me.

Randy grinned and began digging in his pockets.

"That was back in the day," my son commented, pulling out a neatly folded set of ones, fives, and tens. He set them on the table. "Food costs a little more now." His grin was getting wider by the minute.

"It doesn't cost that much more," came Jess's reply, his tone sarcastic. "And seventy-seven wasn't back in the day. It happened to be a very good year. Not too long ago either."

In the meantime, my jaw was dropping to the floor. And I almost dropped Randy's plate with it. These two men, who as far as I knew had never met, were talking to each other like long-lost cousins. Had I been kidnapped by aliens or something? When had Randy and Jess ever met?

"W-when . . . ," I was cut off before I could get started.

"Juanita, you'd better set that plate down. You're about to drop it." Jess turned back to his pancakes. "Better be some fives and tens in that roll, Randy."

"Yes, sir," came the muffled reply.

I set the plate down on the table, my eyes narrowing as I studied my son. He grinned and ignored me and picked up his fork. I turned back to Jess.

"Excuse me . . ."

"And I want to see how you make that smothered chicken thing you were telling me about on the telephone," Jess continued as if I hadn't said anything at all.

Mignon flew by me with a tray of coffee cups and milk glasses.

"Jess has been looking forward to meeting your son, Juanita." She went by so fast I felt a tailwind. "He's kinda cute, you know."

"Excuse me?" I began again.

"I tried to make those dumplings you described but they turned out like chewing gum so you'll have to show me." Jess set several plates on the counter for pickup.

"Ummmm . . . no problem," Randy answered, chewing on a piece of sausage that he had stuffed into his mouth. "I adapted an Amish recipe. It's not really hard. You just have to make sure that you don't handle the dough too much. If you do, they get tough."

Well, was someone going to act like I was here at all?

And since when did Randy know how to cook?

"Excuse *me!*"

The entire diner turned to look at me. My son and the love of my life both turned to look at me like I had landed from the moon.

Jess's eyes twinkled. It only made me more pissed off.

"If I can interrupt this happy reunion . . . just when did y'all get to know each other?" I turned to my son, hands on my hips. When he was ten, this used to strike fear in his heart. I could tell it wasn't having the same effect now.

"Lord, Juanita, that's old news," Jess answered, grinning. "Randy called here collect one day looking for you. I think you and Millie went to Missoula or maybe that was the day that you and Mignon went to the Joann Fabrics looking for kinte cloth." He stopped and peered into the saucepan where the grits were simmering.

"You didn't find any, did you?"

I stared at him. Mignon was giggling again.

"Find any what?" I asked.

"Kinte cloth," Jess replied, his lips curving upward into a smirk.

"Jess, that is not what I'm talking about."

He shrugged his shoulders nonchalantly. "Anyway, Randy called. You weren't here. I accepted the charges and we got to talking."

"Found out we have a lot in common," added my son, who was now gulping down juice that I had squeezed last night from tangerines, oranges, and lemons.

"We talked about food . . ."

"And that's another thing!" I was almost yelling now. And there were just too many grins going around.

"Where did you learn how to cook?" I asked my son. "You never even turned on a coffeepot."

Randy smiled.

"I learned a lot of things inside, Momma," he said evenly. "Most of what I learned, I don't think I'll need outside. But the cooking part . . . well, I kinda like that."

"And that smothered chicken dish sounds all right to me," Jess chimed in, giving those grits a stir.

"That's what I'm talking about," Mignon flew by me again.

"Listen, I want to know . . ."

I didn't get the next word out. They were off and running without me.

"Now be sure to use Lawry's seasoned salt on the chicken," my son advised, raising his finger in the air to emphasize the point. "It adds just enough flavor to the dish."

"I . . ."

"OK, and the parsley in the dumplings, not on the

chicken, is that right?" Jess asked, jotting down something on a notepad on the counter.

"Um-hum . . ." Randy answered. "But not too much. You don't want 'em to look like they came from the Emerald City."

Jess's eyes narrowed as he studied Randy over the top of his reading glasses.

"I think I know how to garnish a dish, *boy*," he snapped back.

Randy shrugged.

"Just thought I'd let you know . . ."

"Let me tell y'all something . . ." I interrupted. These two good old boys had something going on that I just hadn't picked up on.

Jess gave me the evil eye now.

"Juanita, you gonna stand in the middle of the floor and pontificate forever? Or are you going to eat up your breakfast and get over here and mix up that Italian pasta salad you were going on about? You know Violet Mason's quilting circle is coming over here for lunch at eleven-thirty." He flipped the notebook shut and turned back to the grits, ladling out a huge spoonful. "Must have forgot that pill again," he muttered loud enough for me to hear.

I threw a tangerine at Jess.

And missed.

It split when it hit the floor behind the counter.

Jess's grin was like a spotlight. I could never stay mad at him long.

"Are you gonna make that juice drink by throwing the fruit on the floor or are you going to use a cutting board and a knife like normal people?"

The lemon that I threw hit him right on his butt.

There was so much orange drink left over that I served it to Violet Mason and the girls for lunch.

And Jess and Randy made the smothered chicken as the dinner special that night. By eight they ran out of it.

The crickets were singing up a storm that night. Montana was cooling down and the evenings, once softly cool and quiet, had become the stage for singing critters using all octaves. I couldn't believe that summer had come and gone. I couldn't believe that my son was actually here beside me.

"What are you doin' out here?" I asked Randy once we were alone, sitting on Jess's back porch swing. The yellow porch light cast a warm glow on Randy's face. I couldn't resist, I reached up and stroked his cheek like I had when he was little. I was surprised when he didn't swat my hand away as he would have done only a few months ago. "What made you decide to come?"

"Well, when I got out, it seemed like the thing to do," he said matter-of-factly. "I didn't have anything else planned for a month or so. And besides, Jess sent me the money."

I shook my head. I was still trying to get over that.

"We had been talking on the phone off and on for a few weeks. When I told him that I was getting out, he said I ought to get a change of scenery. Sent me the money for a bus ticket and food. All I had to do was show up at the Greyhound station."

He paused for a moment as if he was thinking about something. Then, I realized that he was looking at a fawn and a doe who were standing on the ridge, barely visible in the waning light. They were looking out over the cliffs. I could tell from his expression that he hadn't seen anything like this before.

"No one ever did anything like that for me," Randy continued, shaking his head. "Only you, Momma. But nobody else. Not my father . . ."

I looked down at my hands. I had just turned eighteen when Randy was born. His father had seen him only a few times in his life and had made himself scarce after I went to court to try to get child support. I felt bad about that and I said so.

"Momma, don't worry about that. You did the best that you knew how. What I'm talking about is that this man I never met before treated me like I was his son. He and I talked like we'd known each other for a hundred years. And he was into cooking. It felt good to talk to a man like that. About life and real things and not be . . . not be afraid to say what was on my mind."

I was nosy. I wanted to probe and ask him what had been on his mind but I decided not to. As much as I found it hard to reconcile, Randy was a grown man now, not my little boy. Some of his thoughts had to be his own. And the ones that he shared with Jess, well, I realized that maybe those weren't thoughts I needed to know about. Maybe he needed someone like Jess to share them with.

"How long are you planning to stay, sugar?" I asked, wondering how much time I would have to bask in the glow of this newly formed man.

He chuckled.

"I can only stay about ten days, then I have to go back. My job starts in three weeks."

"Job?" My voice squeaked.

Randy chuckled again.

"I know, I know. You probably never thought I'd have a job. But I got one. I'll be the chef's assistant trainee at Le

New Orleans over on Rich Street. I'm also going to Columbus State. I'm in the advanced food preparation program."

My mouth dropped open. A job.

And school.

And I thought I wouldn't live long enough to see this boy get turned around.

"I'll be staying at the apartment until I can save up a little money," he continued quietly, talking and stopping to listen to the birds calling out to each other as they flew home to invisible nests in the dense forest. "Then I'm going to get a place of my own. Someplace quiet."

"Rashawn's music getting to you?"

He shook his head.

"Naw. Rashawn doesn't get to me. He's a knucklehead, but he's my brother. I just . . . I've been living surrounded by other people for so long, I'd like to have some real peace and quiet for a change."

I had started to say something but now I was quiet.

Randy and Rashawn had been as thick as thieves, cut from the same cloth. Or so I had once thought.

Now it sounded as if I was wrong about that.

"Is he still . . ." Sometimes I couldn't bring myself to say the words.

"Yeah, he's slinging," Randy answered the question that I couldn't ask. "But he's on borrowed time, and I've been telling him that. He won't listen, though."

A low "who who" pierced the darkness.

Beside me, Randy's body tensed.

"What was that?" He looked around, his eyes wide.

It was my turn to chuckle.

"If you weren't such a city boy, you would know." I pulled his ear. "That's an owl."

"Man . . ." he said. There was wonder in his voice. It was nice to hear it there.

"So, you're headed to California next month."

It was a statement, not a question.

I took a quick, deep breath. And I bristled a little. I knew that I would have to say something about this sooner or later. I had hoped it would be later. I wasn't ready yet. California was something that I felt I had to do. Now, with Randy here, the water was getting muddy. The old fears and my doubts about myself rushed back.

Should I go? Should I stay? Should I go back to Ohio with Randy?

"That's OK, Momma, it sounds like a good idea," came my son's verdict. "Don't go back home. Rashawn will drive you crazy."

"Well, maybe I should. He may need me."

"Momma, Rashawn won't turn around until Rashawn wants to turn around. And that shit won't happen until he hits the floor. And hits it hard."

The owl hooted again in the darkness. Randy's body tensed.

"That's what happened to me. I hit the floor. And then I decided that I'd better do things another way."

I knew he was right. Rashawn was as hardheaded as they come. He wouldn't change just for fun. And he wouldn't change just because his momma said so. It would have to be more dramatic than that.

But there was always Bertie. And I told Randy that.

He chuckled.

"Momma, there's nothing wrong with Bertie, 'cept she's lazy."

"She's pregnant, too, Randy, don't forget that. I could probably help her . . ."

Randy's laughter startled a little critter that had been sneaking around the porch. We heard it scurry away through the grass.

"Momma, Bertie wasn't pregnant. Just fat! All that beer, the potato chips, and sitting on her butt all day. Once Dr. Jefferson told her she wasn't pregnant . . . well, you should have seen her! She was off that couch in a flash. Said she didn't want to be a fat ass all her life! She's working back at the Kroger, doing customer service. I'll keep Teishia until I go to work at two, then Aunt Kay said to use the woman who keeps her granddaughter."

I should have known that my sister would know someone. She knew everything. I wondered aloud why none of this stuff had come together before. Why it had taken so much time, so much grief, and so much frustration, not to mention the near-death experiences that Rashawn kept putting himself in.

Randy shrugged his shoulders and stood up, stretching and cracking his knuckles.

"It was just time, I guess," my son mused, yawning and scratching his back.

I thought of all the sages, philosophers, doctors, and shamans who had pondered these questions and come up with the phrase that everything happened in its own time. And now I could add my son's name to that list.

Chapter Seventeen

Randy went back on the Greyhound over a week later. I had to fight with Jess to pay for his bus ticket. Of course, he and Randy had worked all this out beforehand and I was fighting for nothing. Lord, that man is stubborn!

Which is exactly what he said about me.

"Juanita, let me do this, OK?" he growled at me. I wasn't intimidated. Jess was always growling at me.

"He's *my* son," I shot back, handing Randy a small stack of bills. Randy passed them right back to me.

"It's been taken care of, Momma," he said with a huge grin.

"Randy, take the money and do what I say," I tried to play the bossy mother role. But I guess I was getting too old for that. Or was it Randy who was getting too old?

"Momma, I already have my ticket."

"Day late, dollar short, Juanita!" Jess said, sniffing with a superior and smug expression on his face. He folded his arms proudly across his chest. I sighed.

I was outnumbered again.

And I liked it.

Randy left on a Saturday afternoon. He took a couple of Jess's sauce recipes (including sauce Juanita) with him. He left his smothered chicken recipe behind.

I stopped looking over my shoulder after that. I finally realized that my old life wasn't going to come looking for me.

I didn't stare at the rising sun anymore with a sense of fear because I thought it was the messenger of doom bringing me a note from my past that said:

"Juanita! Who do you think you are? You take your butt back and pick up that sorry life you had and don't give me any back talk!"

Now, as I watched the sun cross the sky and set in the west, I didn't worry about my past anymore. Life goes on.

Even my life.

And my children had moved on with their lives—without me. Guess they would have done that sooner or later, but it helped that I moved out of their way. My progress had made their progress possible.

And even though Rashawn hadn't changed his ways, I had changed my way of thinking about it.

That made all the difference.

One day in Paper Moon is pretty much like the next.

Oh, as September moved into October, the breakfast crowd thinned a bit since Mr. Ohlson and the teachers went back to work. But otherwise, everything stayed pretty much the same.

And today wasn't any different.

I got up at five, stubbed my toe on a book I'd left on the floor; cursed at my stupidity and took a shower. Dressed quietly in the dark and listened as the forest woke up. Put on the coffee and stood on the porch to drink it and watch the sun come up. I decided to walk to work. Figured that the exercise would do me good.

The mornings were cool now and Jess was buried beneath the quilts. I wiggled his big toe and he growled at me.

"Be there by seven or your omelet will be as hard as a rock," I told him.

"Hummph!" he answered.

I pulled at his toe again.

He kicked at me.

The mountain was alive with noise and activity. The animals were so busy, they didn't even notice the funny-looking, two-legged creature in their midst with twisted hair on her head going every which way and a tote bag on her arm. Even the deer hardly gave me a look. There were a few other homes up this way, but I didn't see another human form until I reached the highway.

Opened the door at six-fifteen sharp and heard heavy breathing and a slipping, sliding sound coming toward me. Dracula nuzzled my hand. I petted him on the head.

"Good morning, handsome, did you have a good night?" The dog yawned in reply. I opened the door to let him out. Looked around the floor of the diner. "I hope you didn't leave any presents for me like you did yesterday."

Dracula sniffed and seemed to frown at me as if he was insulted that I would insinuate such a thing. I laughed and scratched him behind the ears.

"Get out of here."

He padded out and bounded down the porch steps.

I clicked on the radio and sighed. A country and western tune came through the speakers. Someone had changed the station on me again. Probably Mountain when I wasn't looking. I let it go. Hummed along with Patsy as she talked about "Sweet Dreams." Put two pots of coffee on and went to the refrigerator to get some eggs.

Jess's omelet was getting cold by the time I finished stirring up the pancake batter, frying up three pounds of bacon and four pounds of sausage, and stirring up a pot of grits. Had just popped some toast when I heard the squeak of the front screen door. I'll have to oil that thing, I said to myself.

"Whatcha know, Juanita?" yelled Abel as he and the boys fell into the diner with the same grace that the Marx Brothers had in their movies. The morning went on as usual from there.

By seven-thirty there were twenty people sitting around the diner in various stages of breakfast from coffee and doughnuts to steak and eggs. Mountain came in and ordered the works; Mr. Ohlson, the school principal, stopped by "just for a minute" and ordered a sweet roll, coffee, and fruit (said he was on a diet); and even good old Bobby Smith sat at my counter with his elbows out to his sides throwing down a bowl of grits with enough butter in them to choke a cow. I threw out Jess's omelet.

By nine, the diner was bursting at the seams. The restaurant license gives us a capacity of sixty—there were at least seventy-five people crammed into the place.

"Where's Jess this morning?" Peaches asked with her mouth full.

"I don't know, but I threw his omelet out," I told her as I filled her coffee cup.

"He called fifteen minutes ago, Juanita," Mignon shouted at me as she flew by. "Said he had something he had to do."

I shrugged my shoulders. I wouldn't worry about Jess. One way or another, whether he was late or early, he always managed to be right on time.

"Is Millie coming over this morning?" Peaches asked.

I laughed.

"Are you kidding? Millie's a night owl. She never even comes out of her rooms until noon. Never goes to bed until three or four in the morning."

"Oooooo," moaned Peaches, her eyes widening as she swayed from side to side like a seasick spirit. "She stays up late to commune with the ghost!"

Mignon, Mary, and I laughed, not only because Peaches was so silly but because what she was saying probably wasn't too far from the truth.

"Elma Van Roan approves of what you're doing," Millie told me the day before when I stopped by her room early in the evening. I didn't ask her how she knew that Elma approved.

"Elma wishes that she had been able to be such an independent thinker. Maybe she could have avoided the tragedy in her life."

I shrugged my shoulders.

"I don't know if I'm such an independent thinker, Millie. It's just that, well, I don't want to go back to the kind of life I had before. I guess that means I have to go forward. Even though I'm scared to death."

Millie smiled like a cat that had swallowed the canary.

"Remember what I told you, Miss Juanita," she said, sounding like a prim Victorian schoolmarm. "Always do what you are afraid to do. Your life will be much richer that way." The Siamese jumped onto her lap and purred. "Elma Van Roan agrees."

"Well, I guess if she says so," I told her.

I mean, who am I to argue with a ghost?

"Juanita, I got all your stuff loaded," Carl interrupted, wiping his hands on his apron. "Bobby Smith helped me." He grinned. Bobby Smith was practically my best friend these days.

"Now you remember to eat. I got one whole chicken in the cooler, along with salad, fruit, and bread," Mary ordered, sniffing a little.

"Momma cooked all night," Mignon added, putting her arm around her mother's shoulders. "She's got enough food there to feed you, Peaches, and the army for a week."

"It was the least I could do," sniffed Mary again. She looked at me with bright, wet, light brown eyes. "I'll miss you, sister. You see the world and come back home. Soon." She hugged me tightly.

I pulled Mignon's braid, then pulled her to me.

"Bye, stinker."

"Bye, Miss Juanita. Don't forget. You're supposed to call at least once a week."

"Yes, ma'am."

"And if you don't like California, call us and we'll come and get you."

"Yes, ma'am."

"And don't get out there to Hollywood and party all the time. You're getting to be an old broad and you need your rest!"

"Mignon!" Mary gasped in disapproval.

"Yes, ma'am," I agreed, grinning.

I was getting to be an old broad, wasn't I?

"And please, please come back to us," Mignon whispered, her voice catching.

I hugged her again.

"I will, little one, I promise."

"Where the hell is Jess?" Abel growled, looking around.

I kissed and hugged everyone in the diner—all seventy-five plus of them. From Carl to Fish Reynolds, from good old Bobby Smith to Reverend Hare. Peaches asked again if I was going to call Jess, but I didn't answer her. Jess and I had said our good-byes all night.

No more words were really needed.

Even though I did want to see his quiet eyes again.

The whole crew stood in the parking lot as I climbed up into the cab of Peaches's huge purple rig. Carl pushed the door shut. It started to rain a little. I heard thunder in the distance. A storm was coming. Rolling in from Idaho again. As Peaches pulled around, everybody in Paper Moon it seemed stood there and waved at me.

Everyone but Jess.

Peaches turned the rig around in the parking lot so she could head out toward 90 North. As she did, I noticed Jess, for the first time, climbing a ladder that was in front of the diner sign. It was hard to see but he seemed to be covering the sign with a banner or something. At first, I couldn't make out the letters. Then as Peaches roared by, I rolled down the window.

I read the words: "Juanita's Place."

And I watched the rain dancing on Arcadia Lake until the tears drowned out my sight.

ABOUT THE AUTHOR

Sheila Williams was born and raised in Columbus, Ohio. She attended Ohio Wesleyan University and is a graduate of the University of Louisville. Sheila lives with her family in Newport, Kentucky, and is working on her next book. *Dancing on the Edge of the Roof* is her first novel.